ON
EXHIBITION

ON EXHIBITION

Dale Forbes

Copyright © 2000 by The Reid House, Inc.

Library of Congress Number: 00-190406
ISBN #:   Hardcover   0-7388-1653-1
           Softcover   0-7388-1654-X

All rights reserved. No part of this book may be reproduced or transmitted in any form or by any means, electronic or mechanical, including photocopying, recording, or by any information storage and retrieval system, without permission in writing from the copyright owner.

This is a work of fiction. Names, characters, places and incidents either are the product of the author's imagination or are used fictitiously, and any resemblance to any actual persons, living or dead, events, or locales is entirely coincidental.

This book was printed in the United States of America.

To order additional copies of this book, contact:
Xlibris Corporation
1-888-7-XLIBRIS
www.Xlibris.com
Orders@Xlibris.com

FOR MY FATHER AND MOTHER.

1

My father died between Christmas and the new year—nobody knows exactly when. He was alone. It took some time to find him, and more time to find me.

When the phone rang I was in the kitchen, head down, elbows to knees, examining the chipped floor. I was lucky. If I hadn't answered, the coroner would have worked his way down the contact list, eventually coming to my mother. If she'd gotten the call the instant-epic of my father's life would have been lost to me as well.

My mother was back East, and not in a good temper. My brother, who was hitchhiking through Europe, hadn't cared to mention the stash of narcotics he needed to sell before coming home that Christmas. When he told her he wanted to skip the holiday she icily informed us both that she would be at her sister's, if we cared to call.

I did call, and found her mood had sunk from miffed to murderous. She was less than fascinated by my aunt's friends, but also frustratingly unable to hold her own in the constant tattle of whose husband was president of which major company—or whose child had graduated from Radcliffe, been accepted to the bar, or gotten advantageously married.

She was from old money—raised with the assumption of status by blood—and she was mystified at the thought of having to justify her superiority. But however ill-equipped for social climbing she may have been, my mother was formidable. The flock of veteran debutantes must have watched her cautiously, until she eventually departed, picking traces of wool from her teeth.

Fortunately, my mother was still an unsafe target to snub, but

I wondered how long this would last. My brother and I were absolutely no help in buoying up her leaking life-raft of acceptability. Put in Homeric terms our tales of conquest might amount to theft of chickens and small craft jibing in light wind. My brother's marketing skills, though genuine, were unmentionable. I attended a small western college, got average grades, and held a traitorously democratic volunteer job. Speculation on my marriage prospects would have amounted to complete silence. To my mother's increasing gloom, I had no love life at all.

Not that I was friendless. I had two housemates—Sandra and her boyfriend Roger. Both had departed before Christmas, leaving me alone in the rundown, beige and green rental we shared in Colorado Springs. The phone was in my name. That's how the coroner found me.

His first words, "Are you the daughter of Lewis Pierce of Hailey, Idaho?" sounded like an accusation.

"Yes." I admitted.

I didn't know what to say when Mr. Stanford tactfully informed me of my father's death. I had to look at a map to find the nearest airport. Hailey appeared to be in the exact center of Idaho, one road in and one road out—ten miles south of the famous ski resort, Sun Valley.

I was surprised at the quick sympathy offered by the travel agent when I explained I needed to fly to Idaho to settle my departed father's affairs. I was not used to having a father, let alone getting sympathy for losing one. It appeared to me that loss had happened many years ago. I thanked her and went calmly to pack a few things.

Ripples began to form in my calm when I got to the airport. The travel agent had booked the flight, getting me what the airline called a "bereavement fare." There was a problem though. With no direct flights, I was scheduled to catch a connection in Salt Lake City. But with all the skiers traveling to Sun Valley, there was some uncertainty about the availability of a seat.

As I stood in the lobby at Salt Lake waiting standby for my

flight, the agent told me I would not be able to board and would have to wait for a later connection. Right there at the counter I burst into tears, sobbing brokenly until threatened comfort made me retreat. I sat down, still undone, staring at the plastic chairs in the commuter section of the terminal. My fragile journey was stalled; I was stranded in unexpected grief.

A few moments later the agent came and got me. I jumped as he intruded on my landscape. Wearing a concerned smile, he gently informed me that there was a seat after all. I assumed they bumped someone else from the flight, not wanting a hysteric on their hands in the lobby.

It was a short flight, and I was still shaken from my public outburst when the plane touched down. I waited while the other passengers deplaned, looking out at the forbidden state of Idaho. Back in Colorado Springs, I had decided not to tell my mother about Lew's death, or that I was going to Hailey. I felt confident that I could handle it then, but now I felt out of my depth. I wanted help.

I called her from a pay phone in the airport lobby, my fingers sweating. As she picked up the phone my back went cold, but I said fairly calmly, "Lew Pierce died."

She was silent for a moment, then she said: "Well?"

"I'm in the airport at Sun Valley."

"What are you doing there?" Her voice was sharp.

"I told you. The coroner in Hailey told me that Lew Pierce died in his home last week."

"What is that to you?"

"We have to do something—there will be things to take care of. I think I need help."

"I've always told you to stay away from there."

"But Mummy, he's dead! What harm can it do?"

"You have no business there, and I'm already sick of talking about this."

"But Mummy!"

"Get back on the next flight to school where you belong. You have work to do." I was silent and she continued. "If you stay there, you'll have to suffer the consequences on your own. You're making your bed. Lie in it." It was one of her favorite expressions.

She hung up.

I do not come from a family of gentle people.

The green-suited rental car clerk gave me an interested glance, tugging the bill of his matching hat even farther down. I thought disjointedly of an exotic shellfish whose peering eyes had captured the centerfold of *National Geographic:* a Perna mussel. The clerk checked my license and narrowly informed me that one of my parents would need to sign for the car, as I was not yet twenty-one. I hadn't thought about that. I already felt too old, but it was going to take another three weeks to be old enough. I lied, telling him I'd look for one of them.

Outside the emptying airport, a taxi driver with a ponytail and sunglasses leaned on the door of a yellow Pontiac parked between snowdrifts. His was the only taxi left in the queue. Most of the other passengers had already departed, hauling their mounds of luggage and gaudily bagged skis into waiting cars. He was sunning his back in the steeply-angled afternoon light. Catching my movement from the corner of his half-closed eye, he turned and looked in my direction.

I screwed up my courage, hefted my thin backpack to my shoulder and approached him.

"Can you take me to the Sawtooth Chapel?"

"Somebody die?" His face became distant for a moment. I guessed he was replaying the last few days of local gossip, trying to remember a death.

I made some noise, not truly verbal, hoping to bring his attention back to me without actually having to answer him.

"Sawtooth Chapel? Sure. Get in." He didn't offer to take my backpack. I slid into the seat and dragged it after me.

The ride didn't take long. I paid him with my credit card. He shuffled in his wallet while I waited and handed me a rumpled business card, along with my receipt.

"That's my number."

"Thanks."

I stuffed the receipt and his card in my shirt pocket and watched him drive off.

The chapel was a one-story brick building with snow hanging off the roof. A neatly shoveled walk led to two separate entrances. One looked rather like a garage door; the other was flanked by a small statuary. I chose the more formal of the two. Three concrete steps took me to an entry adorned with small, somber, indecisively Christian artifacts. An empty bench stood rigidly against one wall. Hesitating, I pushed through the windowed door to the second room. It had a counter like a hotel lobby. In back a computer lay silent. In front were several chairs and a low table.

I sat for a moment, then walked up to the counter and looked into the back room. I made a little noise, scuffling my feet. I could hear a radio in the very back playing country music, but no other sign of life. Somewhat anxious that I might cause a fuss by demanding attention, but more afraid that no one would be there anyway if I did, I sat back down and waited. There was no third option.

At length the back door slammed and a rather tall middle-aged man appeared. He started to wash his hands in the wall sink and jumped when he noticed me, clearly having thought that he was alone. He rallied instantly to ask, "May I help you?" Drying his hands on a towel.

"I'm Lew Pierce's daughter."

"I am so glad you could come. I'm Charles Stanford. We spoke on the phone." He put down the towel and extended his hand. I knew from my initial contact with him the day before that he was both a funeral director and the coroner of Hailey.

He excused himself for a moment, returning with a file, a man's wallet and a set of keys. He invited me to sit again, and settled himself into one of the chairs. He placed the wallet and keys on the table, then scooted the wallet a few inches closer to me. "Your father was apparently in the habit of carrying a good deal of cash."

I was too oblivious at the time to wonder why he was proud of this fact, and it did not occur to me to be grateful for his honesty.

He laid the file down. "I am very sorry about your father's death. I am afraid this will not be particularly easy for you, but of course under any circumstances these things are not simple for the survivors. Your father died at home, alone. There were no witnesses, no records of what happened. Because of this, we must perform an autopsy." He added delicately, "The body was not discovered for some time and this makes some tests impossible. We must do the best we can."

He looked at me, gauging my silence and state of mind. Apparently satisfied that I was holding up, he went on. "I need to know the names of the surviving relatives so I can inform them of the death. I also need to get some idea of your father's state of mind in the weeks before he died. I tried not to disturb his house, because it is rather unusually kept, and I felt you might be of some help to us here."

If I was not overwhelmed before, I was headed that way now. "Other than my mother and brother, I don't know who the family members are," I replied, embarrassed to admit the full scope of my ignorance concerning my father. Then I was quiet, sure that explaining would teeter me over the edge of the discomfort I was experiencing. I glanced around the room again, feeling alone and not very competent.

Mr. Stanford stirred in his chair and suggested helpfully that my mother might have some more information. When I said nothing, he drew a series of papers from the file and passed them over the low table for me to read. They contained information on the services of the chapel, and a few forms. I looked at the bottom of one and saw my father's signature. Strange; it was so normal, not large, slightly decorative. Very legible. I glanced at the document. It was paperwork donating my father's body to the University of Utah's medical school.

I said, somewhat frantically, "How soon before we have to give him to them?"

"The medical school?"

"Yes."

"Your father obviously wanted his body donated to science. But I am afraid that will be impossible because of the time that elapsed after his death and before he was discovered. We are not entirely certain yet, but it was at least three days." He looked at me guiltily. "The medical school only wants bodies within twelve hours of death."

To myself I thought, with relief, *Good thing.*

"Well, in any case, nothing can be done until we establish the cause of death, so there will be time to decide all these things." Mr. Stanford's interest changed course abruptly and he asked, "Has your father's lawyer contacted you?"

"No."

"That would be a good place to start." He paused. "It was necessary for us to go through your father's desk to find out who needed to be contacted. Your father's lawyer's name is Judy Crawford." He wrote her name and phone number down on a piece of yellow paper and handed it to me. "We found out about you from his will." Another pause. "How long has it been since you have seen your father?"

"I can't remember."

"Oh."

2

I was three when we left Idaho, old enough that I should have remembered my father. I've often found it strange that my recollection should slide on this one crucial point, for it has captured so many other scenes from the past. Through my childhood these visions buzzed, like prisoners of fly paper—stuck at random angles, troublesome and sad, but no longer meaningful.

From early on I accepted that having two parents was not to be my lot. Strangely, I could recall expressions of faces opposite my father and the smallest details of my situation after we left him. Just past babyhood, during ominously expanding nights, I recall gazing toward the dark entry of my small room. The door was firmly shut and, as the moments stretched, I longed for rescue. But if my equally troubled father entered to hold me, then I cannot remember. It may have happened.

I do remember the man who taught me to ride. His fleeting image, though far from blameless, caused me no grief. The rancher stands clearly in my memory, a gray-haired man with frosted chin and cheeks. He seemed huge to me as he lifted me to the even-taller horse. His weathered barn was the closest one available to my mother, and this was important because she could not escape the affairs of two small children, and what she deemed a very part-time husband, for long. She was always in a hurry.

We lived in a mobile home park. What was to have been our home was still under construction. It lay several miles south of town, just a mud lot with an outbuilding or two, the foundation newly poured. My patrician mother was desperate to get out of the trailer, away from my brother, Franklin, and me. According to her, she was largely unassisted in the daily chores of parenting by my athletic and alcoholic father.

Raised by a nanny herself in the upper floors of the family mansion outside Boston, my mother could not fathom the role that marrying a ski-instructor had cast for her. She was comfortable with a borrowed British model of parenting, about as relevant to her current situation as the moth-balled debutante gowns stored carefully under the direction of her father on the third floor of the New England estate.

She had neither baby-sitters nor nanny, never mind the space to house any help. This small Idaho town accommodated a ski resort like a pony carries a fat man. Post-thaw in those days, there were virtually no activities for upper-class women. Streets ran with mud as water from the slopes percolated through the town. In front of the flow the parade of tourists migrated back to Boston, Chicago, Los Angeles, and New York.

It appeared that my mother made the best of it for a while. Pilgrim stock is tough. But after a few warm seasons of desperation, she decided to take up her own childhood summer hobby of horseback riding. I imagine my father must have objected at first, desisting only at the thought that she could think up worse amusements. The partner she selected for purchase was a spirited palomino gelding with a copper body and creamy mane and tail. She named him Blondie and as the mud dried spent increasingly more time at the ranch that housed him.

She had not much patience with the demands of children, and perhaps afraid of what might occur in the tiny house trailer if she stayed, my mother went to great lengths to leave us with any willing neighbor. When freed, her Brahmin blood stirred her to volunteer work as well as to take pastoral rides through the aspen-clad hills. No adulterer could have expanded time more creatively than my guilty mother. She returned stealthily to the trailer court, justifying her hours away with amplified good works.

In truth, she did help establish a luxurious new library, and worked on the fund-raising committee to create a hospital. She had borne my brother and me among cast legs in one of the infirmary rooms, perched in the upper floors of the Sun Valley Lodge, and considered it uncivilized.

But a proper hospital or a new library could not mend my parents' marriage, which was doomed from the start.

My parents first met when my mother was in her late twenties, unattached, and vacationing in Sun Valley with her engaged younger sister. My father, in his early forties, had already served two decades with the resort after the war. I am not sure of the exact circumstances of their meeting. To question her on this subject has never seemed advisable. But probably he gave her a ski lesson.

According to my grandmother, my parents indulged in what should have been a brief affair. That might have been the case, if my mother had not come back East and found herself pregnant. Months later when she returned to Sun Valley with the desperate news, my father did the right thing, or what seemed like it. I was the afterthought of their passion, born in the winter, two years after my brother.

According to my mother, becoming a family man was not in my father's list of aspirations or attainable skills. He may have assumed that my stricken mother would take care of parenting, as his mother had. He continued skiing. Raised in relative poverty and occupied by a job that granted as complete fulfillment as he could imagine, he may never have realized what a house trailer and unfinished mud lot would mean to my mother.

Arguments between them must have been commonplace, impossible to resolve, bitterly fought. Eventually my mother put my brother in kindergarten and took me with her to the barn, leaving me with a gray-haired rancher-turned-riding-instructor, while she went off on her palamino. That the clever-handed old man had certainly shocked, and possibly deflowered, most of the older girls attracted by his horses was something that my mother may not have known. In any event, my first experiences in the stable included more than just riding.

To give him credit, his pedophile's bargain was not one-sided.

I hated the rowdy families down the street where ragged, competing children hung like aging moss out of trailer doorways. I would have accepted more than mere fondling in order to accompany my distant mother. I remained shyly speechless with the gray-haired man, while my mother rode happily. He was not cruel.

My rancher wisely chose as my first school horse a docile and perfectly trained gelding, named Buckeye. He was aged, as the horse people say it. That means some indeterminate age over ten. He was dark brown in winter, and in the summer, dark bay. His slight star was covered by a long forelock; two modest white socks decorated his hind feet. His movement, clumsy and short by horse standards, filled me with borrowed strength and mobility.

My mother bet the old man that he could not teach me to ride by myself.

"It is impossible," she said. "She is too little to pay attention."

The rancher planted his cigarette in the paddock soil with his boot. Grinning, he answered: "You just watch, Missus, she'll do fine."

The small western saddle was just right for a toddler, the horse obedient and patient. Within a month the rancher had pocketed my mother's wager and given me the foundation of skills that would carry me through many troubles. But he was not my father.

3

I wondered if the old rancher was dead, too. Mr. Stanford at the funeral home politely gathered up the paperwork from the low table, indicating the few places where my signature would be required. I knew about legal documents, and read through them carefully. A disclaimer from the funeral home, release of liability, acceptance of personal effects, then finally the permission to transport "the remains of the deceased."

I asked, "Where is my father now?"

Without hesitation Mr. Stanford answered, "We have a fairly well-equipped mortuary here."

"You mean he's here?"

He nodded, silent for a moment, waiting for me to continue.

"Can I see him?"

"I'm not sure that would be a good idea, though normally, you understand, I am a great believer in family members' viewing the deceased; but in this case you see, the condition of the body was, in a manner of speaking, unstable." Here his professional interest fought for a moment with his better judgment, but he continued: "You see, the body goes through several predictable stages after life ceases; and he was lying in a heated room after all, which hastens the process. Really, it would be better for you to remember him as he was. . ."

I took a deep breath and infuriatingly, as I let it out, tears started to slide down my cheeks, rapidly running off my chin into my empty hands. The coroner tactfully handed me a box of tissues, which I ignored, feeling as if he were receding as my loneliness took the high ground of the scene. He moved as if to touch my shoulder and I virtually leapt to my feet, moving off to the other side of the room, gauging the distance to the door.

Thankfully, the funeral director moved away, saying in a conciliatory way, "There's really no hurry, and as I have said, an autopsy will be necessary. I am afraid you will have a lot to keep you occupied. Do you have any family here?"

"No."

"Well, I am sure you can call someone and get help. That would be the best thing to do. Get some help. According to the law firm, Mr. Pierce named you as executor of his estate, but that doesn't mean that you have to do everything by yourself. Are you of age?"

"No."

"Well, we will have to ask the lawyers about that. In fact, I believe your father named a second, if you were unable to perform that function. Where will you be staying while you are in town?"

I looked at the keys and the wallet lying on the low coffee table. It was suddenly clear to me that I wanted to go back to my father's house, be among his things. I was in fact desperate to be there.

"How far away is his house?"

"Not far. It's just to the north of Hailey, about halfway to Ketchum on the west side of the highway." Looking at my slight and irrational movement toward the door, he added hastily, "Would you like me to take you there?"

"Yes."

"All right."

Mr. Stanford picked up the thick wallet and stack of paperwork, along with the keys, and gestured toward the door.

Hesitating only momentarily, I preceded him. The late afternoon had turned to twilight while we talked. I looked back, inquiring about where to go. He gestured past the newer white Suburban to a foreign pickup with an aluminum camper top. As he walked toward the truck it started to rock a bit, and the low sound of a large and happy dog came from the back of the vehicle.

He lowered the tailgate and affectionately greeted a very robust German Shepherd, who worriedly licked his face and then pointed her large ears in my direction. He bent down and placed my backpack carefully next to her, closing the tailgate and window as she obediently backed away.

"Her name is Sadie. She's only a few weeks away from whelping, but she still likes to come along," he volunteered.

We got in the truck. It was strewn with maps and contained a flashlight and a rifle in a gun rack. Mr. Stanford signaled, then pulled out of the driveway and headed left, to the north. He turned on the radio, the same country station I heard in the Chapel. After a while he slowed, searching for a road sign amid the snowdrifts.

A semi truck skimmed past on the off side, barely slowing and dousing us with a spray of water from the melted snow. In a few hours it would be ice. Mr Stanford negotiated the turn and then drove more confidently the few blocks to my father's home. We pulled in the driveway. He got out first and walked to the back of the truck, waiting there for me to emerge. Sadie whined and wagged her tail loudly against the aluminum camper shell. That spurred me to action and I reluctantly opened the door.

He asked, "Can I let her out?"

"Of course, Mr. Stanford." I was surprised by his requesting permission.

He smiled at me. "Nobody calls me that around here. Chuck will be just fine."

Sadie lumbered out of the truck, greeting me with a quickening enthusiasm, licking my hands and whining, wagging her tail energetically. She was happy to be out. Greetings accomplished, she ran between the sizable snowdrifts and had a quick pee.

Chuck was standing in front of the pair of faded blue doors, sorting through the ring of keys. The doors faced south; the sun had melted the ice in front of them, and the entry light revealing packed mud, faintly dusted with fine, dry granules. I realized someone must have shoveled, because there was a lot of snow piled around that looked relatively fresh. I wondered who had done it.

The house was tall, brown stucco with a lot of windows and a simple roof line. It was not frightening in the slightest; yet more than anything, I felt like running away. I was in the middle of regretting my choice to stay when Chuck found the key and opened the right-hand door. He led the way in, feeling for the light switches.

The air in the room was stale, but not grotesque, as I had imagined it would be. The pieced-together carpet showed no saturation or visible stain from the passing and patient waiting of my father. There was, however, not a lot of carpet to be seen. The vast room was filled with a maze of waist-high artifacts, with paths like animal runs snaking through them.

In every possible location, barring the shelves, the stuff flourished. Piles of mail cascaded off bags of canned groceries, which leaned passionately against ancient blenders and newer but dust-encrusted food processors. Power tools and winches were adorned with unopened bags of paper napkins. Cans of beets festooned with nails, acted as shelves for medications and wood scraps. Soiled rags and hand tools cohabited with cleaning equipment. The room was flanked on all sides by cabinets, but they sat uninhabited except by sawdust.

Toward the right, in the kitchen area, lay piles of some white substance with little black specks. It filled Styrofoam cups, overloaded plastic plates, drifted off the counters and onto the floors. I'd never seen anything like it. It was crumbly in some places, round in others. It looked faintly geological, the older piles having accumulated a thin layer of dust.

I sat down in my father's chair, which was mercifully clear of debris.

Chuck said, "It is possible you'll need a Dumpster."

Overwhelmed, I considered Dumpsters for a while, gazing out over the rolling sea of effects.

Chuck went to the door and called Sadie, then went outside, presumably to help her back into the truck. I realized he would be leaving soon. Slightly panicked, I moved abruptly from being shy of Chuck to dreading the idea of his departure through the blue doors, leaving me amid the chaos of my unknown father's house. I got up and hurried to the entry.

He was carrying my thin backpack to the house. My mother would be even angrier if she knew how quickly I had come. In her eyes, this would be further evidence of my thoughtless and ill-prepared character.

"Did you have anything else?"

"No."

He set my bag down next to a large tank that looked like an air compressor.

"What was it you wanted me to find again?" I asked, deciding to ignore the fact that finding anything specific in this house was going to take a very long time.

"Shall I write it down?"

"Yes, please."

Chuck took a pen from his shirt pocket and found a scrap of paper. He pulled up a white plastic lawn chair and cleared a space for its legs with his foot. Then he settled at the desk to write. After a few moments he was done with his list, but he did not hand it to me. Perhaps he was not ready to go.

I asked him finally, "Can you tell me how my father died?"

He leaned back a bit. Clearly, he had done this many times. The concerns of the living were possibly as predictable as the changes he expected from the dead; the timing of the questions varied, but not the content.

"We'll have to wait for the autopsy to find out exactly what happened, but I'd be glad to tell you what I have seen and think, if that will help."

"I think it might."

"I got a call from the police asking me to meet them here last Thursday. It was the day before New Year's Eve, the 30th. Hailey is a small town. You know from our conversation yesterday that I act as both funeral director and coroner. I'm called automatically whenever anyone dies outside the hospital, or under unusual circumstances.

"The local police were already here when I arrived; I asked them to leave things as they were. As I have said, this is a small town. We are, thankfully, not used to many dead bodies. Anyway, there is a tendency to move too many items. Even if the police don't need to know how things were, the family does. We only needed to do routine site photos before we transported your father's remains."

"There will be other formalities?"

"Not until the autopsy is complete. Then we'll see. But I think we will find nothing."

"No?"

"No. The police were called when the man who reads the gas meter looked through the window and saw your father on the floor. The door was locked and he ran next door and called for an ambulance, though it was far too late for any help. The sliding door on the west side was not locked, so once they had dug around to it, they didn't have to break in. Anyway, your father was lying here, in front of the main doorway, in his coveralls and snow boots. There was no sign of violence or struggle; it all looked relatively normal. But, as you can see, his housekeeping was not usual, so it is difficult to tell."

"You mean, it's hard to see if things have been disturbed."

"Yes, exactly. But really, we have no reason to imagine anything but natural causes. Your father was not expected to die for some time, but these things are often unpredictable."

"He was ill?" I asked.

"Yes. According to the doctor I spoke with at the Veterans' Hospital, he had lung cancer. I called them after we saw his veteran's card. The actual records are in Boise."

"Oh," I said.

It looked like the funeral director was ready to go. He got up, and behind him the list fluttered aimlessly to the ground, almost immediately camouflaged in the ubiquitous litter of my father's floor. I was tired and resigned. I walked with him to the door.

"The autopsy is scheduled for tomorrow. After that we will have more information. Shall I call you?"

"Please do."

"Are you going to be all right here? Do you want me to take you someplace else?"

"I'll be fine," I said, doubting it.

There was no place else to go, no way out but through.

After he left I tentatively began to explore my father's house, trying to see what order might be lying beneath the expanse of debris. The vaulted living room was traversed by several huge beams, giving a branched effect. The house began to cool as darkness truly fell.

I thought about my folly. It was immense. Asking Chuck to leave me in a house I knew nothing about was truly stupid. I did not know if the heat, phone or anything else worked properly. Worse yet, there was no way to escape if things did not go well. Simply trusting fate, I had blundered to Idaho, irritated my mother and potentially caused a lot of trouble. As the magnitude of my incompetence hit me, I found my naiveté anything but charming. If there was trouble, I no doubt deserved it.

Reluctantly I checked the phone, not expecting it to work, absurdly certain that, mimicking my father's death, it would have shut down. The dial tone clicked on. I looked at the receiver for a moment before replacing it. There was no one to call. I heard a rumble and was frightened for a moment, but it was just the furnace turning on. Almost instantly it warmed the structure and then quietly subsided.

I looked for a bathroom. I found one downstairs by walking through a narrow bedroom. I took one look at the encrusted toilet and retreated. I found a bottle of spray cleaner next to some oatmeal and drill bits and carried it in for a first assault. Standing with the bottle adjusted to "stream," I soaked the toilet and the carpet around it. Moving backwards out of the room, I emptied the bottle. Then I took a deep breath and went outside to pee.

Venturing inside again, I made my way up the open staircase. I passed power tools and stacks of canned goods. My father had apparently used the stairs as much for storage as for ascending to the loft. His sleeping area waited.

The floor by the large and rumpled bed was littered with magazines, the selection dominated by *Playboy* and the occasional *Hustler*. Down the open hall, past a sauna, lay the upstairs bath and laundry. I stripped the filthy sheets off the bed, noticing a large group of rags covered with blood and spittle lying on the floor. My father had been truly ill.

I cleared the top of the washer of a huge pile of clothing, noticing with surprise the same towels that I grew up with. White, though in this case gray with dirt, and a blue monogram. I picked some up and deposited them with the sheets and blanket in the machine. Several boxes of detergent lay off to one side. I remembered several more near a cache of soup downstairs.

The machine obediently started to cycle as I turned the dial, and then there came the vibrating sound of a pump underground. The water was hot, rushing into the washer in a steady stream. I let it play over my hands while I leaned on the rim, looking down as it soaked the sheets. A group of slim white hairs emerged at the surface of the turbulent water. I looked again and they were gone. My throat tightened, a lost child uncomfortably revived.

I had missed my dad.

Instantly, shreds of other memories appeared, reassuring as a rapist haunting a familiar window. The furnace murmured again downstairs, the heart of the house muttering, still working, simply missing the creator, whose face I struggled to recall.

I walked back to my father's bedroom, wiping my eyes, and sat down on his bed. I looked down at the collection of magazines on the floor, remembering my mother's cautions, trying to steel myself. On the rare occasions when my brother or I would timidly ask about our father she had become shrill. Mention of him would provoke a burst of criticism. He was a dangerous man: violent, intemperate, alcoholic, selfish, irresponsible, a man capable of financially abandoning his children without a second thought. Had we ever had a birthday card from him? Had he made any effort to support us in any way? There was proof positive that he did not love us and was not worthy of any of our attention. In any case, people of his moral character were not the sort we had been raised to associate with. She expected more of us.

So, talk of my father had been limited to allusions that he might hurt us if he ever found out where we lived, or that he was a drunk. I was ashamed of the word divorce, hating it when strangers asked about my family. I took to saying simply, "I have no father." Once, the belligerent younger brother of a friend pressed the point, sneering: "Well, who made you born?" The young man was hustled from the room by his mother as I flushed, trying to think up an excuse for my mother's version of the immaculate conception.

Sitting on my father's bed, my tears drying, I looked down at his reading material and thought my mother had a point. As Chuck said, I needed to procure a Dumpster. I would then dispense with this filth. It was utterly foolish to be miserable about the death of a man whom I could not remember and who, in all likelihood could not have cared less about me.

After a while I put the sheets in the dryer, made my way downstairs and looked for something to eat. I opened the refrigerator and quickly shut it. Though it appeared to be running, the odor from within was grotesque. I would deal with that in the morning. There were, however, many cans of beets stacked around and these looked safe. In fact I liked beets.

I hunted around for a pan. My father had a good supply, arranged around the house in the manner of talented children playing hide and seek. I don't think I caught them all. The oldest were the same as my mother's, but differently sized. I imagined they were from the same set.

Looking in the sink, I saw that my father had recently eaten from the same plastic bowls my brother and I had used as children, later replaced with fancier china by my mother. Apparently the squall of my mother's final departure had left many objects at sea. In one manner or another my father incorporated these articles into his life, adding to them over the years, but never abandoning them. Somehow, this lent me hope.

4

When I was a child, as evening came to the West, the phone would ring. As my mother picked up the receiver, my brother and I would begin a migration to the bedroom. We both knew that the living room was not safe after the phone was back in its cradle. As my grandfather sang siren songs over the lines to my mother, my father stewed in the car. The old man's nightly consultations from the East undermined whatever life my ill-suited parents might have made together.

When my mother put down the phone, my father's voice would rattle the walls of the house trailer. My mother's voice was generally quieter, but it was frightening when we did hear her, because there would be a scuffle. She might cry out, sometimes in rage, less frequently in fear.

Always after these fights our father left, slamming the door. Then we could hear her softly on the phone again, the noise of his car fading. When the realities of the life she had chosen became too clear, the East coast must have loomed in her mind like the promised land over the horizon.

In any case, my grandfather was a hard man to compete with. An industrialist and reputedly a fine judge of men, he had been hired by "Wild Bill" Donovan for the Office of Strategic Services during the second World War. Living in Washington for most, though not all, of my mother's childhood, his task was to recruit agents. He harvested talent from the promising stockpile of the young, upper-class offspring of his business contacts: men and women anxious to serve their country, but bored by the thought of traditional service. He found plenty of volunteers.

I am told that he grieved the too-routine disappearance of his young protegees keenly, but when all was said and done his character was eminently suited for this kind of work. The war intensified his innate passion for manipulating people's thoughts and actions. It provided a power unequaled by his experiences in business.

My grandfather stayed in Washington for several years after the armistice, helping to mop up and to stabilize the communist entrenchment in Eastern Europe. When he returned home, his almost-grown children, and eventually their spouses, became his game pieces of choice.

He apparently came to abhor my father for his stubborn refusal to take advice from his betters, so he cut off funds to my mother. The family fortune was not to be squandered by the arrogant and uneducated. If she suffered while she maintained this contact, then so be it. My parents' house lay unfinished, snow piling in the foundation. Finally my mother had had enough.

Our trips to the barn became abbreviated as she packed boxes gleaned from the grocery store. Before my father came home each evening, the closed and taped parcels were mailed. Box by box she shipped her possessions home; then, one gray afternoon, she loaded my brother and me into the battered station wagon and drove south, over the Snake River, to Twin Falls. There she established herself briefly in a rented suburban home, waiting for her divorce. When it came, documents signed, we headed back East, leaving suddenly, as had become my mother's habit, too early in the morning to have eaten, with her glancing in the rearview mirror.

My mother's small convoy consisted of two children, two horses, two cars and the horse trailer. Her first employee after the divorce was the driver of the horse trailer, a man recently released from jail, but as my mother later put it, only for stealing from the government and everybody did that. My grandfather had at any rate checked him out, and dubbed him safe.

"Mummy, I want to go home," I said, thinking thankfully of our trailer, my large-handed father and the two striped kittens we had left behind.

She nodded. "We'll go home in a while."

She claimed it was so, but we never went back. The horse trailer relentlessly followed us, but the big-handed man, for whom she looked in the mirror, was not in pursuit. Perhaps he was at home making breakfast. There was no sign of him anywhere.

My mother's flight back East terminated at *her* family home, a large, brick mansion placed on a generous plot of land. Here, she and her sisters and brothers had been raised, with full aid of staff. But on the day we drove up the circular drive, my mother was thirty-three, the majority of the servants long dismissed. The remaining staff included only a full-time handyman-gardener and a cook.

At the sight of children the household instinctively reverted to its old routine, with or without adequate help. My grandparents, who were strangers to my brother and me, made us welcome, immediately ushering us to the nursery on the second floor, which consisted of a suite of gray rooms at the back of the house.

It was spring, and the windows looked out on a sea of blue scilla bulbs growing low under the shade of pine trees. The painted twin beds on the far side of the nursery were made of wrought iron. As children, my uncles had been tied nightly to these thin white railings, preventing escape until rescue at sunrise.

My mother deposited the horses in a local barn, dismissed her hired felon and settled back into her spawning ground as an adult. My mother's new room, formerly occupied only by guests, was in the front, facing west, as were the other formal rooms. The third floor children's quarters were closed. My brother and I later found the house contained five more bedrooms. My mother, her brothers and sisters had graduated one by one to the third floor from the nursery as they had become teenagers.

When not in boarding school, the children had occupied this upper story in private, occasionally pushing open the trap door to the widow's walk that crowned the roof line. The view from this height was dizzying. Each of the children in turn had practiced walking the circumference of the roof, eyes straight ahead, balancing precariously on the thin railing of the windswept walk. They lived semi-independently from their occupied elders, who never knew of this activity.

In years past the eastern view from the widow's walk had included a glimpse of the inland harbor. My female ancestors had leaned on the rail looking east to the water, watching for the return of their husbands or brothers aboard trading ships from the Orient. The regular arrival of these ships, their holds packed with tea, ceramics and silk, traded for Indian opium, had established my grandmother's family fortune.

The trees had grown now, obscuring the glimpse of the ocean. My grandmother, born years after the China trade ended, walked the roof only for pleasure, taking breaks from her social work to look west across the broad lawn and the forest beyond.

Following her mother's example in the thirties, my grandmother happily crusaded for birth control rights. Ironically but perhaps persuasively, she towed her five children along to visit the Catholic poor. She was not the sole liberal generated by her family. Her mother had been a suffragette whose political forwardness rivaled her daughter's. This line of intelligent and stubborn women worked for social causes as a career. Making the world a better place was a duty. Their dedication lasted for lifetimes.

My grandmother vehemently disliked visiting the network of new social contacts my grandfather was anxious to cultivate. She bit her nails as she paused in her typing and despite relentless walking her figure was matronly. She seemed not to care. Her patrician discomfort with flashy affairs was innate. She had no need to go visiting. Making small talk had little appeal, and her social standing—if she thought about it at all—was assured by both her name and her stout backing of worthy causes. My grandfather, who had ceased pressing her to accompany him years before, was now clearly content to take my trim and lovely mother as a companion.

The first few weeks in my grandparents' house, which I remember with astonishing clarity, were a bewildering mixture of social events and neglect. My brother and I were left every afternoon in the nursery to take an unaccustomed nap, because it was nap time. Our days were filled with the rituals of upper-class child rearing: incredibly regular meals, scheduled playing, walking and sleeping. Orderly, efficient.

A visit with one of my mother's acquaintances or one of my grandfather's contacts was an almost daily occurrence. My brother and I were included in the visits of friends with children, though the children invariably were not present. The guests were anxious to view the fruits of my mother's five-year absence.

My brother was forced to endure a haircut in order to make him presentable. The crew-cut Franklin looked like a small and stubborn five-year-old marine. My nondescript but willful three-year-old hair hung around my face unnoticed.

One afternoon during a nap Franklin, not at all sleepy, took his blunt scissors from the art kit and invited me quietly to play "Haircut." Sitting on the second twin bed, he happily snipped away the hair on the entire left side of my head. My mother interrupted him before he could complete his job, her face lengthening and solidifying as she looked from the bed to me to him. She took the scissors from his hands and soundlessly hacked away the hair on the other side of my head. We were then taken downstairs for a snack.

During the next several months, as we were introduced to her old friends, my mother may have regretted giving me a unisex name. She had to explain constantly that she did not have two charming little boys. I think she finally made me wear dresses that cool spring to prevent the continual misunderstanding.

After a period of receiving visitors, my grandfather developed a very forward social plan for my reluctant mother. She was to make as many public appearances as possible. This was supposed to advertise her return unscathed from the West. She dressed up daily. The sight of her appearing in the nursery, hair freshly done, long slim legs sheathed in silk, a trim coat draped over her shoulders, became commonplace. After a quick kiss goodbye for my brother and me, she would allow my grandfather to usher her out.

We were left at home with my grandmother and her absolutely essential cook. My grandmother, an extremely well-bred New Englander, never got the knack of the kitchen. She could barely make a pot of coffee, let alone a complete meal. The household would have starved without Molly. Neither woman was much interested in the affairs of children.

The cook was Scottish and, unlike others of her guild, extremely thin. She was also busy, and did a lot of heavy breathing and bashing of pots whenever we got near the kitchen. One morning we amused ourselves stealing peeks at her from the stairs and giggling. She stormed past us up the back stairs, rounding the corner to my grandmother's second floor study with a full head of steam. She found her employer mid-hallway and blurted out her complaint.

"These children! They are underfoot all the time. I can get no work done!"

"But Molly, imagine if we had eight children, or ten! They really are not a bother." We certainly spent no time at my grandmother's doorway peering and giggling. She went on, "We have a woman flying in from the West to interview as a nanny this Wednesday."

The cook, seeing the blank wall before her, retreated, while muttering, out of my grandmother's earshot, "Ten children and we'd be an orphanage!"

My grandmother instructed my brother and me to play in the playroom and not bother Molly. Then she returned to her work, occasionally checking on us, establishing that shoes were mandatory and that running was to be done only during the walk she provided every afternoon. She did not dislike children; she simply had no interest in them until they were old enough to carry on a conversation.

My brother and I were allowed freedom in the playroom, which contained a miniature wooden barn with a large selection of carved animals, a lot of blocks, books, and a piano, which we were forbidden to touch. We were used to spending time together and playing alone. The volatile nature of our household in Sun Valley had attuned us to the moods of our elders. Watchful, but not particularly frightened, we adapted fairly well in the first weeks.

My mother would sometimes take me with her to check the horses. This made me happy. Blondie and Buckeye were housed in stalls, instead of their normal pole-paddocks. The new barn had a long, neatly swept concrete floor. There was even a man teaching riding. He wore baggy pants and tight boots. When not on a horse, he was surrounded by a flock of dappled, glistening young girls.

One day, watching the girls ride, I asked him, "May I ride too?"

He replied, "No, you're too young."

I could feel my eyes grow hot. I looked at my feet with shame, but I knew he was wrong. I had ridden by myself down the road to the mailbox on Buckeye almost every day in my western saddle back at home. Too shy to argue, I said nothing.

My mother led me around sometimes as I begged her to set the horse loose. The older girls had English saddles and jumped poles set on little fences. I was passionately jealous.

5

I got the sheets from my father's dryer and made his bed. Though it was late, I was keyed up. I hunted for suitable reading material and found a stack of black-and-white magazines downstairs, with fuzzy pictures of skiers in old clothes. These looked relatively safe. I opened the first one at random. The cover picture was of a man dressed in a white parka, wearing glacier glasses and carrying a rifle strapped to a sizable backpack. The front said, "Blizzard." It was a newsletter from a military outfit called the 10th Mountain Division. I was in the middle of thinking cynically, *This ought to put me to sleep*, when I started to wonder why Lew had a bunch of these in his house. But then, what did he not have in his house? I read on.

The 10th Mountain was a division created in World War II and had fought in Italy at a place called Riva Ridge. Not much mention of combat during the rest of the war after that, though from what I knew, the war had lasted for another year.

The second newsletter contained a long article on training in 1943 at a place called Camp Hale in Colorado. I read others. In the back of each issue were chapter notes from different areas of the country. I found one from the Idaho and Montana region. It read: "I visited our famous scout, Lew Pierce, while driving North from Boise through Sun Valley this summer. He is ornery as ever, busy building a house, and said he'll be at the next reunion as long as we keep it on this side of the Atlantic."

Near the middle of the pile of newsletters, I opened an issue and a pair of stapled Xerox sheets fell out. On the first page was a picture of a good-looking, dark-haired man in his thirties. He held a ski pole or shovel diagonally across his body, clasped by large hands. The man was looking past the camera, smiling, lips closed, but friendly. My father.

The author of the article was Todd Smith. I had heard of him, founder of *Smith Outdoor Equipment*. They manufactured ski poles, bindings, and goggles. In an article about skiing in Sun Valley, the writer was probably the same man. It was from the local paper, the date was almost ten years before, February. I read quickly through the article, then read it again.

> There's a quiet, modest, unassuming, gray-haired man among us who, in an activity peopled by thousands of superb performers, was arguably the all-time best skier in the world. But let me backtrack a bit. In the 1978-79 winter, an old friend, Nick Howe, from Sun Valley's 1953 Ski Patrol, visited me. In the course of some marvelous reminiscences dating back to even before Sun Valley existed, he told me he'd been traveling the world looking up people who'd figured prominently in skiing history.
>
> A high point, one might guess, was a visit with Emile Allias during the 50th anniversary celebration of Emile's triple gold medal performance. Emile, for those of you younger readers who don't remember, was one of *the* giant figures in modern skiing. As a racer, he dominated his era. As a coach he taught James Couttet, who at 17 won an Olympic downhill.
>
> As an instructor, Emile was the major force that popularized parallel turning. As an instructor and ski school director on three continents, he simply electrified every area with which he was associated. And, as an area planner he was responsible for several striking and innovative resorts in the French Alps. Still an active and remarkable skier, he's "seen it all" for at least 55 years and is as knowledgeable about all aspects of skiing as anyone, living or dead.

> Well, my friend asked Emile, 'What skiers stand out in your memory?' His answer was, 'There have been so many, so many through the years. But there was one American I remember, he was not a racer or even a well known instructor, but he could ski so well. More than that, he skied the same in every condition: smooth pack, deep powder, bumps, ice, slush—anything. That's the mark of a truly superior natural skier. His name was Lew Pierce. I always remember him, one of the best.'

I stopped for a moment, flushed with pride in my father. Then I read on.

> Before he could mention any others, the conversation turned to the old days at Sun Valley. Would he have named Haug, Erickson, Pravda, Molterer, Sailer, Killy, Thoeni, Stenmark, etc.? We'll never know. Suffice it to say that from the Pantheon of skiing all-time greats, Sun Valley's Lew Pierce was the name that leaped to his mind first.

> Consider that Emile has seen and probably skied with almost every great racer or outstanding skier in the world ever since the early 1930s. He hasn't even seen Lew since 1961, but Lew immediately popped into his mind. He didn't even name any alternates.

> Locals from the 1948-50 days will of course remember their awe at what Lew could do on skis when he arrived at the resort. A couple of examples: the Harriman Cup downhill was set down Olympic one year. After the cat track and the springboard, you were on your own—no control gates on The Meadow, then a hard right fall-away turn onto Steilhang at maybe 50-60 miles per hour. Unweighted skis couldn't possibly hold the turn, and the racers who were packing the course protested to Nelson Bennett, the course

setter. U.S. and foreign, they were all standing at the top of the Steilhang, the best racers of their day. All of them thought it couldn't be done without a control gate or two in the Meadows.

Benni turned to Lew and said, 'Show them how to take it.' Lew climbed up to the top of the Meadows on skis and, without even stopping to catch his breath, shot straight down the Meadows, made a hard turn at the bottom, and pulled up to a stop in the narrow, V-shaped gully. He'd never pretended to be a racer, but he humbled the best of them that day.

There were follow-up notes on the next page from people across the country. One read:

Smitty did not mention that Lew was on 7-foot-3 (220cm) wood skis in the '50s, very unforgiving off packed runs. On a pair of Brunetto's light and short 205s, Lew would have looked like Fred Astair dancing, coming down Exhibition or Inhibition in crust breaking around his ankles. My pick for the absolute best all-around skier was the same, Lew Pierce.

I put the papers down. My dad had been a great skier, a star athlete, respected. Where was the violent, frightening, dissolute man my mother had described?

6

Perhaps it would have been a kindness in that vast brick New England house to continue the tradition of tying children in bed at night. A few weeks after my haircut, something woke me early in the morning. A door closing? I lay in the darkness, listening to my brother's quiet breathing. It was cool in the room, the first hint of light showing through the window. I waited silently listening for the noise. It did not come again.

I was restless. My grandmother had given me a mechanical stuffed toy the day before. If you turned the little key on its side, it walked a few steps and then made a cat noise. I knew I had left it in the playroom next to my grandfather's study. I thought of it and imagined it in the little pretend bed I had made. I talked myself into the fact that it had woken up too. Grownups would sometimes believe this kind of thing.

I was not allowed out of bed before the grownups, and certainly not before full light. With great care I slipped out of bed, the plastic soles on my pajama feet scraping slightly on the wood floors of the hallway. I sat down at the top of the stairs and looked down onto the landing and entry below. There was a bit of light outside now, but the shadows in the entry were still deep. I might have lost courage and crept back to bed, but there on the table next to the front door sat my mechanical cat. I knew that was not where I had left it. Its bed was beside the piano in the playroom. Toys were not allowed anywhere but the nursery and the playroom.

One by one I slid down the stairs on my bottom, very careful not to make a noise. When I got to the last one I hesitated a moment, eyeing the coveted cat just a few steps away. As I stood up, stretching my hand toward it, the door to my grandfather's study opened. He emerged fully clothed, and didn't look at all surprised to see me.

He asked, "Why have you come here?"

I was already guilty of being out of bed, and my cat was not supposed to be out of the playroom. Not knowing what else to say, I replied, "I want my cat." I didn't think he would believe it had woken up.

My grandfather walked over to the table and picked up the toy. He turned it over and glanced at the protruding key. I thought for a moment that he was going to give it to me and, smiling with relief, reached out my hand again to take it from him.

He did not extend his arm, but instead said, "You should not be up."

I looked at the floor, my hand dropping. I said, "I'm sorry."

My grandfather said nothing, but walked over to the stairs and picked me up. I was becoming somewhat frightened, but was not yet in a panic. I thought that perhaps he would take me back upstairs to my room. I hoped he would bring the cat.

The old man turned, but instead of starting up the stairs he moved down the hall. I could see where his glasses pressed into the side of his face; the gray and thinning hair lay in orderly wisps over his temples. He retraced his steps back to the study. As we passed through the entry, the door clicked shut firmly behind him. I could feel my lips starting to tremble, but as I was about to cry he slapped his hand over my face. The room was terribly quiet. I could see the lawn through the windows, the air opaque with mist and first light.

Walking quickly toward the windows, he deposited me on the brown leather couch. The inner walls of the study were lined with glass-fronted cabinets. Their shelves were occupied by many little figures and objects, little elephants, fans, and boats, all formed of the same smooth material, sharing a milky color stained with little etched details. I thought for a moment even in my apprehension that this must be his playroom, that he had a lot of toys. He approached me and I huddled back against the cushions, bewildered, watching him.

I knew just then, with an intuitive leap of certainty, that I was in a lot of trouble. I tried to get very small, backing into the pillows. He turned away from me, fumbling with his belt, his trousers loosening. Now I was utterly terrified. My father had beaten my brother once with a belt for breaking his fishing rod. Remembering his screams made me lose control. I started to cry, anticipating the sting.

But my grandfather did not remove his belt fully. He sat down, a greedy look showing on his face, his trousers open. He pulled me face down roughly onto his lap. My cries were muffled there. He grasped what was left of my hair, his fingers pressing into my skull and hurting my ears. He forced my open mouth down over the shaft of his exposed penis. Pumping my skull up and down hard against himself, he made small noises as if in pain.

My scream had no sound, for I could not breathe, struggling like a fish in hand. I was quite certain I was going to die. Smothered, choking, I must eventually have passed out, because I do not remember the end.

I awoke in my bed, throat burning; my lip was split and had bled on the pillow. I groggily vomited onto the bed. My weeping was hushed, as I feared he would return. I looked at the mess on my pillow and knew with certainty that if what had just happened was the punishment for walking downstairs before light, then the grownups would kill me when morning truly came. I turned the pillow over and covered my bristly head with the covers.

I was going to die. I awoke a second time with the blood from my mouth streaking the clean side of the pillow. The bed was wet, and there was blood on the sheets as well as on my pajamas. I knew without a doubt that I was the worst little girl that had ever lived. I had been punished, and I would be again when they found me. No thread of outrage tainted my guilt.

My mother cleaned me up in the morning. She was not as mad as I had feared, but clearly was not happy. She told me I was sick, and made me spend the day in my room. My brother had to go on the daily walk by himself.

All that afternoon I shivered under the covers, alone in the room, fear lapping at the sides of the bed like an ocean. My grandmother brought my toy cat from downstairs, looking worried, saying she was sorry I was sick. As my terror sailed unpiloted, I told myself that the covers were magic. If I kept my hands and feet under the blanket, nothing could get me.

Sleeping, I dreamed of hands reaching from under the bed, trying to catch me and pull me down where I would smother in their grip. I awoke and the door to the nursery was shut. I was terrified looking at it, knowing now that a closed door was not safe, but could not bring myself to get up and open it. I knew that whatever was under my bed would reach out with lizard-like quickness and grab me as soon as my feet touched the floor.

In the weeks following my grandfather's assault, I made a metamorphosis, but instead of cocoon to butterfly I went backwards. I became a vile and primitive thing. If called, I would remain stuck, afraid to move and equally afraid to be found. I wept silently in hallways, terrified because I could not find my way back to my room. I lost my toilet training because I could not bring myself to get out of bed before someone came for me.

I do not think I was a particularly difficult child before we moved. My mother was mystified by my behavior; I am sure she publicly attributed it to the move and privately needed to think so. My regression was more than she could bear under the scrutiny of her family. Her self-esteem was in a jaundiced state, already coping with failed marriage, flight home, and a new life to begin.

My lovely mother came to abhor me as a symbol of her connection to damaged things. She left more to myself, which was easy for her to do because as fast as she retreated from me, I fled the inexplicable world in which I had landed. I was sick for long periods, not speaking or playing. They took me to a doctor, who pried my mouth open for examination while I sat shivering and sobbing. In the end he said I had a bladder infection and a delicate character.

I am not sure what would have happened if help had not come to us in the form of a nanny. My mother and grandfather had been searching, but it was one of my mother's leftover friends from Sun Valley who provided the lead.

Mrs. Burns, our eventual nanny, had lived in Twin Falls, not far from our briefly rented house. When we had alighted near her earlier that year, she had been in the process of burying her husband of thirty years. As we traveled east, she asked her friends in Sun Valley about jobs caring for children. It seemed to be purely by chance that she came winging after us within months of our departure.

Mrs. Burns was of firmly midwestern stock: she was slow-talking, ample-bosomed, patient, and indulgent. She arrived the same week my mother and grandfather closed on the purchase of a small suburban farm.

One of her first duties was to unpack our clothes and belongings, mostly still encased in ragged cardboard boxes. She eyed with dismay the state of our expensive wardrobes, as well as of the family linens. Short pencil in hand, she instantly starting a shopping list that included starch.

The new farm was about fifty acres. My grandfather intended it to serve double duty, as a home for my mother and as a general family retreat. The complex included a main house that was built originally in 1714 and had been added onto in a rambling fashion. This large clapboard structure contained seventeen rooms. A second, smaller house for the help was set off to the rear, connected by a covered breezeway where wood was stored. Across the driveway stood a huge old barn with two levels and an enormous loft.

Neglected apple and pear orchards grew on either side of the long, sloping driveway. A spring ran off these hills, feeding a small pond. Beyond the pond a swampy area housed owls and foxes in search of ducks, and farther still a meadow bloomed with an opulence of weeds.

The buildings were as neglected as the farmland. White paint fell away from rotted boards; fencing needed repair. My mother delightedly hired a recently emigrated Canadian named Mr. Saunders as handyman. He and his wife moved into the little house in the back. With my mother in the lead, they set to work revamping the facility.

While they worked outside, Mrs. Burns organized the kitchen and made bedrooms for Franklin and me. She moved into the west wing of the main house, to which we were forbidden entrance by my mother, who wanted to be sure "the help" had some privacy after clearing up after dinner.

Mrs. Burns, in reality, spent very little time in her inner sanctum. Too gregarious to make use of her time off, and lonely without her adopted family, she set out determinedly to spoil me and my brother with little attentions. Instead of small adults, we were treated like children. She provided songs, games and general cosseting. My rather more serious brother did not know what to make of it, and was embarrassed by the attention. I loved it. Cuddled on her lap one day, I decided that Mrs. Burns was my real mother.

Though not often in residence, my grandfather was constantly in the background at the farm. He called every evening to go over the day's events with my mother. He was, of course, the major stockholder. My mother's trust supplied ample income, but no meaningful source of capital. He had arranged the money for the purchase, and clearly thought the purse strings were tightly bound to the amusement that her nightly reports provided. Fortunately, he actually visited only on holidays and special occasions. His presence made Mrs. Burns stir around nervously in the kitchen cooking not her usual shepherd's pies or cookies, but more elegant roasts and racks of things.

My grandfather spent almost an equal amount of time on the phone with all five of his children, checking on their lives, discussing plans, plotting and scheming with and for them. However, I always thought, as did my mother, that she was his special chosen child. Only later did I learn that over the years he had invited each of his children into his scrimshaw-lined study to say privately that he or she was his best and favorite. Naturally they were all expected to succeed given that they had his special attention and support. He orchestrated their every move.

My mother asked him one day, in my hearing, about my father's alimony checks. The family's discreet and ancient law firm had done a fine job for my mother in her divorce. My father, who most days could not afford lunch, was directed to assist one of the wealthier New England families in providing for his children. The Idaho courts awarded a level of support several hundred dollars in excess of his total income. This, on top of his legal fees, crushed him. As his debt grew, he took to drinking in a truly serious way.

In any case, according to my grandfather, my father's paltry cash was not an issue for us. Still, my mother was curious. "Are the alimony payments still coming?"

"He must have quit his job. Might be drinking again."

"What about the money?" she asked.

"You just let those payments pile up. That way if the bastard ever tries to use his visiting rights you hit him with the bill. It's cheap. Forget the money; it's not the point. Keep your number out of the book and your name out of the paper. You'll never have to see him again in your life."

My mother smiled.

7

That first morning in my father's house I woke up mad. My mother was selfish; my grandfather was a pervert; and, even if Lew might have been the best skier in the world, he was an incredible slob. Standing amid the clutter, I wanted to grab my backpack and get on the first flight back to Colorado. My mother was right. This was not my problem. I stomped barefoot to the upstairs bathroom and jammed a toe on Lew's clutter. "Damn it!"

Then I looked out the window. What I saw took my breath away. To the west a treeless, snow-covered mountain reflected the rising sun. I went to my father's bed and lay down again. Propped up with a pillow, I watched the color of the mountain fade from rose to yellow to white as the sun climbed to full morning. Lew had watched this every morning. I wondered about the name of the mountain, and the location of Exhibition and Inhibition, the ski runs mentioned in the article. I would have to find out.

That window was cleverly placed.

In fact, as I looked at the design of the house in the morning light, I realized that the whole thing was cleverly done. The cabinets were not of fine wood, but they were handmade and beautifully constructed. The staircase, curling up to my floor, was suspended from one huge upright beam, the shaped stairs carefully fitted in a spiral. Huge windows took up most of the walls facing the mountains, and mirrors in strategic places amplified the light. There were essentially no doors, yet the house felt private. How had I missed this oddity yesterday?

The mirrors were placed in such a way that there was no area in the house where you could not see behind you. I liked that. Nor was there a drawer or cabinet that was without its special function. They had been constructed with a plan. I wondered who Lew had got to build it. Why had he never really moved in, just heaped his things in piles? All the cabinets were empty. Lots of questions wanted answers. I was no longer angry; now I was curious again.

I decided to clean up my father's house, but first I needed coffee. A quick rummage produced three standard coffee makers, two industrial types, six thermoses, four boxes of filters in three sizes, and a case of Styrofoam cups. Five fully sealed three-pound cans of coffee begged to be chosen. It seemed that my father had been fond of coffee as well.

I found Chuck's dropped list and taped it to the refrigerator, thinking, *If it gets loose in this place again it will be like finding a needle in a haystack.* It read simply: "Names of relatives and recent contacts, medical information."

While I made coffee I started looking through piles by the desk, and before long stumbled on a medical section, filed right next to three cans of WD-40, several more drill bits and a bag of crisp marshmallows. That reminded me that I should tackle the refrigerator today, which made paperwork seem like a luxury.

The pile started with a lot of Medicaid insurance notices, documenting payment for recent treatment at the Veterans' Hospital in Boise. That was not too surprising. I put these aside for Chuck and checked them off my list. Down in the stack a bit I found a notebook holding worksheets from an alcohol treatment center. From the dates, he had been arrested for drunk driving almost ten years ago, and compelled to go through treatment.

I read through my father's notes. It looked as though there had been a test. It was pretty clear he was shining them on a bit. His answer to, "Why do you want to stop drinking?" read: "My family is important to me." There were handouts about depression and methods of treatment. I wondered what Lew's forced march through therapy had been like. He had taken a lot of notes and I read his clear script with interest. He sounded like a bright guy. It also sounded as though a lot of that information was new to him; a lot of underlining indicated a high level of interest.

The next series of paperwork included a lot of handouts, which he had apparently also read. The sheets contained a lot of interesting information about anger and how to express it constructively. I came across a series of handouts on Post-Traumatic Stress Syndrome, the fancy label for shell shock. They talked about veterans exposed to life-threatening situations, or witnessing severely violent scenes during combat. These men apparently suffered frequently from alcoholism and sleep disorders.

There was a long article describing flashbacks to traumatic scenes unrelated to the present. A few sections were underlined, but there seemed to be little concrete information about what to do about the problem. I wondered if there was a cure. I wondered how much action Lew had seen with the 10th Mountain? I was not entirely sure what the duties of a scout were.

The coffee had finished dripping. I got myself a cup and spotted the ring of keys, the wallet that Chuck had left. It was weird looking through someone else's wallet. I felt like a thief as I emptied it on a recently cleared table. Hiding behind a VA Medical Center card, a credit card, and a stack of various business cards was my father's driver's license.

I picked it out with sweaty fingers and held it up. A clear photo. There, staring back at me, was a white-haired man. He had striking blue eyes. I knew the color. His features were symmetrical, straight nose, well shaped mouth and strong chin. He was clean shaven, neatly groomed, wearing a turtleneck and ski sweater in the little picture. That was my dad, as an older man. I put it down, oddly shaken, comparing it to the fuzzy photo of him as a young man in the ski article.

After a while I picked the license up again and read all the information. Birthday: January 17th, two weeks away. He would have been sixty-eight. Older than I thought. Height: five-eight; weight: 165. We were the same height.

I returned all the cards to their pocket in the wallet, and guiltily extracted the cash. Almost three hundred dollars. I thought he was penniless, but he carried more money than my mother usually did. It was very strange. I put the money back.

The ringing of the phone startled me. I had to hunt a bit to locate it. I saw it hiding under disturbed papers, red light to the left of the dial blinking as it rang. Looking at the power tools spread around and imagining the noise they made, I understood why he wanted a light on his phone.

"Hello?"

"This is Judy Crawford. I'm Lew Pierce's lawyer. Is this his daughter?"

"Yes."

"I'm so sorry to hear about Lew's death. He was a very sweet guy."

"Thanks."

"Is there anything I can do to help you? We'll need to get together and go over the details of his will."

"I'd be happy to meet, but I'll have to arrange transportation."

"Didn't Chuck give you the keys?"

"Keys to the house?" I was embarrassed. I hadn't looked at them.

"No, keys to the cars. Lew had several cars. I'm sure at least one of them works, because I saw him in town the week before Christmas."

Looking outside at the massive snowdrifts, I realized that they were probably hiding my father's collection of cars.

She continued: "I'll need to meet with you tomorrow or the next day for signatures. I've spoken with Chuck and he tells me that you are under age, but that you look pretty competent. I'll act as co-executor, according to Lew's wishes. It shouldn't be too complicated."

"This is a small town!"

"Absolutely." She sounded amused. "And to tell you the truth, we've all been dying to get a look at you. Lew was pretty well known in the valley, and he talked about you a bit."

I was feeling a little overwhelmed. I wondered if she had ever seen Lew's house.

"What will we have to do?" I asked.

"Probate in Idaho isn't too complicated. We will have to record the will and post several notices, identify potentially interested parties. The whole process takes about six months. There are several legal hoops to jump through, but I don't expect any trouble. Lew thought a lot about what he wanted to do, and the will is clear and properly written. I just tuned it up a few years ago. But we *are* going to need an inventory of all the items in his house."

Eeek, I thought.

The lawyer continued. "He basically left his whole estate to you and appointed you as his personal representative. That gives you about as much latitude as the law will allow. That's bound to make things easier for you. He and I discussed this when he was alive.

"Lew built the house himself and it's unencumbered. He was pretty good with money, and made do on quite little. I know he was living on social security, and when he got sick last year he was very concerned that the cost of his illness, even with his veteran's benefits, would wipe out his finances.

"He very much wanted to leave you the house and he was concerned that an extended illness would leave you with very little to work with. It was important to him. I know he talked with the social services at the veterans' hospital about this." She ventured mildly, "He could be pretty stubborn when he felt like it."

I was astounded, not by my father's apparent stubbornness, but by the fact that he would take any interest at all in me.

"But he didn't even know me!"

"That's not what he said," she replied crisply.

"How long have you been Lew's lawyer?"

"I used to live next door to him. He hired me for a few little things and about two years ago, right before my husband and I moved to Stanley, he asked me to check his will. You were always the beneficiary, but he tuned it up as the assets in his life changed.

Actually, if you want to know the truth, he was sort of obsessive about it."

"Oh," I said.

"We are going to need an inventory of the estate; you know, a list of the contents of the house, how much he has in his bank account, that kind of thing."

"Judy, how am I going to make a list? I can barely see most of it, never mind count it." I felt guilty right away for complaining.

"You can certainly clean up the house and discard things of no monetary value. In fact you'll *have* to discard things in order to be able to do an inventory. I know it's going to be a big job."

"I think I can handle it."

She sounded relieved. "I wouldn't mind dropping by, having a look—that way you won't have to drive. I'll bring the paperwork. What's your schedule?"

"How about tomorrow?" I liked her, and wanted to have some progress to show when she came.

It sounded like someone had walked into her office. She quickly added: "The man who owns the construction company your father used to work for said he and his wife might be dropping by. I think they have a son at the same school you go to. They're nice people, Wili and Carol. Got to go. See you tomorrow."

She hung up.

I realized again what a small town this was. How did she know where I went to school? I looked back on my conversations. I hadn't mentioned it to anyone. I needed a break. I picked up Lew's keys and one of the three snow shovels inhabiting the room, and headed out to unearth his cars.

After a bit of poking around in the drifts, I located four cars in a sort of chronological lineup. First there was a small blue Subaru; next came an older Mercedes diesel; after that a van that looked like it came from the seventies, followed by a station wagon covered by a blue tarp. The latter, missing a windshield, hailed from the vintage of my baby pictures. The first car in line appeared to be the most likely prospect. I didn't really have to go anywhere, but I knew I would feel better if I at least had the capability. Another project.

Behind the cars was a garage with a lean-to outbuilding in back. I floundered over to it and pried open the door. Several old tires lay at angles under the eves. In some spots the interior was stuffed to the rafters with tools and wood. I knew now who had built the cabinets. I touched the smooth surface of what looked like a major planer, but most of the power tools I couldn't even name. There were many duplicates, all with my father's initials stenciled carefully on them. They looked both well used and well cared for. My hand was tingling.

I set to work digging out the blue car. It took only forty-five minutes to free it. That was a good thing, because light crisp flakes of dry country snow filled the air by the time I was done. I wondered if Judy was going to make it tomorrow after all.

The Subaru was crowded and messy, but it had a full tank of gas and started with little difficulty. I put it into four-wheel drive. On studded snow tires, it lurched handily out of its remaining drift. I parked it near the front of the drive in case we were in for a serious storm.

I was about to go inside when a woman hailed me from across the street, walking through the drifts. She was blonde, athletic looking, older than me by about ten years. She looked at me intently.

"My name is Paula—I live across the street. I'm so sorry to hear about your father."

"Thank you. Would you like to come in a moment?"

"Sure."

Her eyes teared when she walked through the blue doors. She lifted her hands briefly to her face.

"Did you know my father well?"

"Pretty well. We moved here six years ago when he was mostly finished with the outside of the house, but my husband borrowed tools from him and they would do projects together. He was a very sweet man. We're going to miss him."

"Would you like a cup of coffee?"

"Yes," she said, starting to look for a seat before I could offer one. She dragged another white resin chair opposite Lew's recliner. It reminded me of Chuck the day before. It was clear that this was where visitors sat.

I went to the kitchen area, retrieved my own Styrofoam cup, and gave her one. Then I sat down damply in Lew's chair and looked at her.

Paula immediately started to cry again. I felt desperately unable to offer any comfort, and sat dumbly. But presently she stopped sniffing and got up in search of a paper napkin, which she used as a tissue.

"I'm so sorry, but we used to do this sometimes, sit and drink coffee together and talk about things. I haven't seen a recent photo of you, but it's spooky—you've grown up to look so much like him."

I was in shock, but Paula went on, oblivious to my amazement.

"Lew used to talk about you all the time. He knew you were in college in Colorado and he was proud of that. He said he missed you terribly."

"But he didn't know me."

"He said you were the happiest little girl on the planet, always giggling. He told me he used to like to feed you breakfast before your mother got up."

In my bewilderment I was starting to cry too. She took this in stride as a natural response, and went on chatting about Lew and the process he had used to build his house.

"Of course, the construction company that he worked for helped with a lot of it. After he retired, the boss, Wili, would come sometimes with the whole crew on slow days and help with the heavy project. But basically Lew did it himself. He would just work along on one thing or another. He liked to be busy. When he got sick it was so hard on him. He hated to slow down. And you know, he had a lot of friends, but he would always go out to see them. Not many folks have been here."

"No?"

"He wasn't much of a housekeeper, was he?"

I agreed, thinking about the downstairs bathroom, still "soaking."

When I walked into the kitchen to refill our cups I noticed again the white substance on the counters. "Paula, what is this stuff? There sure is a lot of it."

"Oh, that! You should throw them away. Lew was saving them—he thought they might be useful for cooking. He liked to bake and he didn't like to waste things."

"But what is it?"

She walked over and looked down at it fondly. "It's hard to tell now—they've broken down a bit. He didn't like the insides, you know, he would scrape the middle out and save it."

"What?" I asked.

"Oreos," she said patiently. "He only liked the outsides of the Oreos, so he saved the middles to do something with. He made a cake once substituting those for some of the sugar and all of the butter. It was pretty awful. Even he said so. But I think he was experimenting still."

"Creative."

"Lew was nothing if not that."

"Paula, do you think it would be okay to throw some of his collection away?"

"You're going to have to!"

"Do you know where I could rent a Dumptster?"

"Sure, Wood River Rubbish."

After Paula left I gave myself a pep talk of truly Puritan standards and tackled the bathroom. I found three and a half pairs of rubber gloves under the sink, two of them still in their original packages. There were multiple bottles of cleaning fluids, almost all with seals intact.

I collected my small battalion of equipment and ventured into the downstairs bath. It was not a pretty sight, still crusty even after being assaulted by cleaner the night before. I set to work.

This job took a good deal longer than digging out the car. After I got done scrubbing the carpet ineffectively with a series of sponges, I found two carpet cleaning machines and three cases of rug shampoo in neat little bottles. They did a better job.

I ate another meal of sliced beets and eyed the impressive stack of scrap lumber leaning against the stairway. Next to it was a table saw. No, two table saws. I decided the best way to find things for the inventory was to put them in places by category—tools, cookware, etc. and to this end I made a series of stacks. The living room looked like a mountain range when I was done. The highest pile was of clothing. My dad had been a clotheshorse.

Halfway through the afternoon I made a phone call. An hour later I unearthed a stereo—actually three stereos in various rooms with a lot of wire. I assembled them on the newly wiped off bookshelves and wired the more likely-looking ones together. Lew had hundreds of records, but the turntable would not function. The CD player was fine. I looked through his selection. It included a lot of classical and jazz. I picked out a Billie Holiday disk and kept working.

Later that afternoon the Dumpster arrived. Four yards of open space, gaping in the snow, wanting to be filled. It was in the right place.

Piece by piece I sorted the old newspapers, shaking each one free of the nails that nestled in folds. At home I would have recycled them, but this was a desperate action. I took most, but not all, of the sixty-five empty coffee cans and deposited them in the Dumpster. The carpet was filled with metal of various sorts. I broke one of the six elderly vacuums when it sucked up too much hardware. Guiltily, I spirited it into the Dumpster, and then found a magnet on a long stick.

Damn it, Lew, why not before I broke the vacuum!

Using the magnet, I easily cleared the floor of two coffee cans of discarded nails. Then it occurred to me. This was a construction cleanup. After a house is built it has to be cleaned before moving in. Lew had been living in a house under construction. He'd just finished the cabinets before he died. They were the last touch. The place was finished. He'd just not had the strength to clean up and move in.

During the afternoon I talked to my dead father, like a madwoman. *"Lew, where would I find a measuring tape? Do you have any more dishwashing soap? How come you have forty pairs of shoes? Which ones do I save and which ones go in the bag for charity?"* The answer to this, of course, was that I saved the ones I liked, because most of them fit me. Apparently our feet were the same size, too. By midafternoon I was finding the whole thing rather companionable, happily pulling on one of Lew's ski sweaters to head out to the garage.

About four in the afternoon I called for the Dumpster to be emptied and sat down. The phone rang as if on cue.

"Hi, this is Chuck from over at the Chapel. I've got some news for you about your father." He sounded worried.

"Is everything okay?"

"Well, we've found some things I'll need to discuss with you. Can I come by?"

"Okay," I said, and he hung up.

I fidgeted, looking at my progress in moving Lew into his house. It was nice to be left in charge, fine to be alone in my dad's home. I hoped Chuck wasn't going to tell me something I didn't want to hear.

I felt tired. The furnace clicked on and I lay down on the sofa to wait.

8

After my mother moved to the farm, she was seldom in the house. She happily supervised our handyman, Mr. Saunders, in building rehabilitation. Mrs. Burns made friends with his wife, living in the small house next door. They called each other by their first names and sometimes cooked together. It seemed that equilibrium had finally been reached.

My grandfather visited us unexpectedly one weekday. Mrs. Burns made lunch. He sat alone with my mother after Mrs. Burns had taken away most of the dishes. I was coloring at the kitchen table, and could hear them through the open door. They were discussing my mother's brother, John. My grandfather's commanding voice made little shivers run over my skin. The crayons wobbled. He said to my mother, "John is at loose ends. He needs to apply himself. He's never going to make it as a teacher. We just needed that excuse to get him through college. You know how he is. I don't want him around my business associates."

My mother replied, "But Dad, couldn't he stay in town and work at the office? There must be something you can have him do; there's nothing for him here."

Mrs. Burns, who didn't like to enter the room when my grandfather was there, moved my book aside and said to me, "Go pick up the water glasses, will you honey?"

I reluctantly passed through the door. My grandfather looked out the window toward one of my mother's partially completed projects. Ignoring my presence as I reached for the glasses, he gave her a meaningful glance. "I think you could use a hand."

Her face got stubborn, and he added, "You'd be doing me a

favor to let him stay. You know how I feel about having him around my colleagues."

Her face softened a little. After a moment she said, "Okay."

I escaped to the kitchen.

Uncle John appeared for several weekend visits shortly after this conversation. He and my mother had Mrs. Burns lay a formal table for the evening meal. Frank and I had to sit with them. There were too many forks. My mother adopted the tradition of ringing a little bell, like the one my grandmother used, to call for the next course. Mrs. Burns was not amused.

These early social occasions brought me to speechless cases of nerves. My uncle sat at one end of the table, my mother at the other, while he lectured us incomprehensibly on table manners, spoke French to my mother, bullied my brother, and told me lies in the name of teasing. My mother said, "You should watch for the twinkle in his eye." Try as I might I could never seem to see it.

I asked Mrs. Burns, "How much older is Uncle John than Mummy?", fooled by his balding crown ringed by still-dark hair. I was horrified when she answered, "But he is your mother's younger brother; your other two uncles are the older ones." I was worried that, being younger, he would automatically live longer than my mother, and in that way come to have even more influence over my life. I need not have worried about the mortality issue; something more immediate happened.

After a short time Uncle John took up residence in one of the many spare rooms. Now instead of the friendly kitchen meals with Mrs. Burns, my brother and I always ate in the dining room with the grownups.

I think my bachelor uncle had secretly complained to my grandfather about our manners. The resultant pressure had come to bear on my mother, and through her, on us. Our various insufficiencies were the main topic of conversation at every meal.

Mrs. Burns and Uncle John disliked each other intensely. One of his main forms of humor was to make insulting remarks about her size when she was out of earshot. Generally, after Mrs. Burns set out the family meal in the evening, she would retire to her quarters. My mother handled the task of putting my brother and me to bed.

Mrs. Burns was substantially built. Uncle John, thinking he was being funny, would imitate her walk as he got his food, swaying from side to side in a parodied waddle. She would barely have shut the door before he would break into muffled pig noises.

My uncle was erratic. One moment he would make strange and obscene noises; the next he would turn deadly serious and scold my brother and me about the correct angle at which to place a fork that was not in use. After this he might decide that another secret conversation in French with my mother was in order, reminding us not to interrupt with a grand, "Children should be seen and not heard!"

Mrs. Burns took to spending more time in the West wing. She patted my back, and invited me to help her write letters to be mailed back to Idaho, sometimes including pictures I had drawn. She said they were for her friends. After a period my mother forbade me to go back there, saying, "Mrs. Burns needs her privacy."

At dinner one evening my uncle announced that he was going to be married.

Many of our neighbors imported their domestic help from Europe. These decorative young ladies often arrived shortly after the woman of the house had become pregnant. Uncle John found these au pairs fine companions. One, a dark-haired English woman in charge of our neighbor's children, was the choice of his heart. Her name was Margaret. She was full-breasted, elegant, funny, and had a wonderful accent. They planned a spring wedding.

Mrs. Burns and I looked forward to the wedding with great excitement. It was to be my first really big party. Margaret's parents were flying over from England, and my grandfather was hosting a reception after the wedding.

My uncle, whose health was suspect for some reason, seemed to be doing well and there was talk between him and my mother of his moving into town with his new bride. Perhaps he would join my older uncles in the family investment business. I was elated. Not only would we get to go to a party, but also Uncle John would leave. Doubtless, we would then return to having dinner in the kitchen.

My mother had promised me a manicure in preparation for this grand event. I actually had no interest in this activity, aside from my undying wish for her approval. To win this honor I would have to stop biting my fingernails. Though I allowed them to be painted with foul-tasting liquids designed to assist this purpose, when the manicurist held my stubby, now eight-year-old fingers she saw, as everyone else, that I had failed miserably. My mother was disappointed, as my nail-biting and general shyness were a source of criticism from my grandfather.

Still, she showed compassion and allowed the process to go on, encouragingly talking about next time. I loved her so much at this moment that I might have died with no regret. For isolated moments she would permit me this adoration.

The wedding did not go entirely as planned. My uncle did succeed in exchanging vows with his wife, standing with her in a massive Boston Church, stained glass windows shimmering light across the alter. But at the party afterwards, a strange thing happened. My uncle had, at the welcome urging of a crisply tailored staff, drunk many long-stemmed glasses of champagne. He danced the obligatory wedding dances somewhat unsteadily.

When the cake was cut the bride and groom stood in front of the crowd, ready to exchange bites. My uncle's hand quivered. He dropped a large bite on my new aunt's foot. As I turned to search for a napkin, thinking to wipe it off her perfect shoe, I heard a loud crash. My uncle was struggling on the floor, lying on his back and thrashing uncontrollably. The guests circled in fascinated horror. The bride turned the shade of her dress and the new English parents-in-law took a step backwards. There was a long hush and we could hear him breathing, and then calls for a doctor.

My grandfather, crimson, ushered some of his more important guests to the other side of the room. My mother stooped by my uncle, giving some medication, looking concerned. The bride sat down suddenly. Eventually Uncle John was helped to his feet. The party went on, but the guests of honor passed rather shakily through the alley of rice throwers and into their waiting limousine. I don't know whether he had told his future bride about his epilepsy.

After a three-month honeymoon in Europe, Uncle John and my new aunt returned, but not to a plush apartment in Boston. It had been decided that they would take over Mr. Saunders' house. With two weeks' notice, Mr. Saunders packed up his wife, a severance check and all his belongings, and returned to Canada. The new couple moved in. Mrs. Burns huffed around for days, writing many letters and cooking only a little. I was sad to see Mr. and Mrs. Saunders go, but thrilled that Uncle John and Margaret were not living in our house.

By this time my mother had expanded the farm to include a boarding stable with eight horses. She hired crews to put up hay, and rode her own horse daily, sometimes joining with the other neighborhood horsewomen to ride over the country, or allowing me to accompany her on Buckeye. She was as occupied and content as I think she was ever to be.

My fecund foreign aunt was almost immediately pregnant. I was terribly excited about the baby. My aunt took a polite interest in me, including me in some of the gatherings with her friends. She was in a slightly awkward spot, having abandoned the ill-fitting role of servant for that of lady of the wealthiest neighbor's house. Nubile, unmarried, unpregnant, she had been every wealthy brood-wife's nightmare.

Now her thickening figure was an asset to her bid for acceptance by the ladies whose children must be her baby's friends. I was something of an advantage, because my presence denoted my mother's tacit approval. So I was taken along.

9

Still reclining on the sofa in Lew's house, I heard the crunch of tires on ice. Chuck was in the drive. I groggily got off the sofa and went to let him in. As he began to knock I opened the door. No dog this time. He got right to the point, refusing the offered cup of coffee.

"The preliminary work for the autopsy on your father was done this morning. We have sent tissue samples off for analysis, but I wanted to tell you right away there is some possibility that he did not die of natural causes."

"What do you think happened?"

"Even with the degradation of the body, it was possible to detect traces of what the pathologist thinks might be poisoning."

"His cooking?" I offered, a trifle flippantly.

I was beginning to feel like Lew and I were a team, and I was irrationally irritated by their prying around in his body. If there was something to know, I was feeling confident that he would have left evidence for me, and that eventually I would find it. Like the magnet for the nails in the carpet. He had left it for me to use. Who else? If past history held up, he was certainly not intending to vacuum. In this case I was not at all sure that he would have wanted the authorities barging in. I felt it was really his affair, even though he was dead.

I tried my best to look cooperative, but I'm not sure it was entirely successful. I said, "You know, it wouldn't make sense to kill a man with lung cancer. All you have to do is wait."

Chuck redirected me. "We aren't worried about murder, but we'll have to record an accurate cause of death for the state. If any suspicion of suicide is suggested things will get very sticky. Do you know whether there's a life insurance policy? It will really become an issue if there is a policy; insurance companies won't pay off in the case of a suicide. They get rather upset about it really. It's considered fraud."

"Certainly," I said," but I haven't gotten far enough into his paperwork yet to know if he even has a policy." I changed the subject. "When was he diagnosed with the cancer?"

"I'm not sure. I'll confirm the date with the Veterans' hospital. They should be sending up the records pretty soon. Sometimes they can be slow. I've only spoken with them on the phone so far." Chuck, still worried, added hopefully, "He was an old man, and sick, probably on too many medications. Sometimes the doctors don't check with one another. You can have an older person taking twenty different pills, some of the prescriptions contradicting each other. People sometimes don't take all of what they are prescribed at once. Then when they feel bad another time they get out the old medications. It can be a real chemical mess."

"When will we have the final reports?" I persisted.

"Possibly tomorrow."

"I'd like to make arrangements to have my father cremated as soon as we can. I'm not very happy with his body being stored in that condition any longer than it has to be."

"Of course. Have you contacted the other members of the family? He will have some relatives that may need to be asked."

Now I was really feeling stubborn.

"I will inform them when I locate their addresses, but his lawyer said Lew left me in charge and that it's ultimately my decision." I could feel myself getting on a soapbox and tried to quiet my tone, "I don't want him to wait any longer than is necessary."

"Yes, you're right," Chuck conceded. He said his goodbyes, promising to call the next day.

I sat down on my sofa again to think. This was a whole new issue. Would my dad consider killing himself? I thought immediately back to the paperwork on depression and sleep disorders. Funny that Lew's reading material did not include any information on the lung cancer he was supposed to be dying of shortly. That seemed odd to me. It also seemed odd that no stories of extensive hospitalization had come up. I'd have to look into it. If the clues were not hiding in his stuff, then I'd have to look elsewhere.

Then I reviewed my knowledge of lung cancer. I knew it was often inoperable, likely to spread to the brain. Victims were prone to seizures through compromised brain tissues. Chemotherapy was the most common treatment. The illness usually lasted from six months to a year and a half when treated.

Still thinking, I glanced outside and saw the empty Dumpster. It was taking the role of a hungry pet. I filled my arms with two grocery sacks of junk mail, a stack of bread wrappers the size of a football, three cans of elderly bacon grease, and a small stack of Playboys. I knew what my brother would say: "Terrible waste of resources!"

And so the late afternoon went, in intervals of careful sorting and gruntingly vigorous exorcism of stuff.

Dusk was well underway when I came across the mother lode. Photos. Lots of them. In a crumpled cardboard box under a stack of catalogues for mail order tools. I sat down instantly to have a look, and right away I knew him. There were probably fifty pictures. Mostly eight by ten, photos that looked like promotional shots from the resort. Very few candids or snapshots. I looked through the professional photos first.

They were black-and-white ski shots and formal pictures of the ski patrol. There was one of Lew as a young man with a Dartmouth college sweater, standing in front of a brick building with four other skiers, lined up for what looked like a yearbook shot. The card in front of them said, "Dartmouth Ski School."

That must have been before the war. He was a teacher. He looked worldly even then, athletic. The thin woman at the end of the line gazed at him in the picture. There was another shot of him standing, in profile, on skis before the view of a valley; a lovely blonde woman, not my mother, stood uphill and laughed back at him flirtatiously. Interesting.

Most of the photos were of Lew and other men. Pictures of the patrol. There was one of a group of men standing on a steep hillside, presumably rescuing an injured skier. My father, unmistakable by now, sturdily anchored the belay line to the stretcher, concentrating on his job. There were pictures of them trudging across windswept bowls, being towed in line by snow cats.

One photo made me stop. A crowd at the base of a ski hill watched the finish of a race. In that crowd, standing half a head taller than the surrounding spectators, was a blonde woman with two children. The boy stood to her waist, the little girl only to her knee, wearing a hat tied under the chin and a snowsuit. I looked back at myself through time in the crowd, very small, standing with mittened hands in the sun.

Under a pile of child's drawings there was something I could not explain: a picture of me in a horse show. It was from a Christmas card when I was about twelve, showing me jumping my feisty bay pony called Trojan over a brush fence. I looked at the photo of my profile. The horse's ears were pricked; my eyes were focussed forward, already concentrating on the jump to follow. I wondered how my dad had gotten it, and what he had thought. Then I thought about Mrs. Burns, picked up the drawings and sat down.

10

One Christmas, just before I turned ten, Mrs. Burns took a longer-than-average holiday, and was not home when we came back from skiing. When she returned, there were several long conferences behind closed doors in the farm office with my mother and uncle. A lot of phone calls.

One winter afternoon not long afterward she told me, tears filling the wrinkles around her eyes, that she was returning home to the West.

"For how long?"

She said nothing and simply cried, patting my back as was her habit.

Distraught by my caretaker's grief, I found my mother in the barn and asked her, "Why does Mrs. Burns have to go?"

Her reply was brief. "Mrs. Burns is getting old. Her children need her. Frank will be away in school this fall, and with only you here during the week we really don't need her."

I couldn't think what life would be like without Mrs. Burns. Meals, laundry, entertainment—all came from her.

My mother held a conference with my brother and me. "Frank will be home only on the weekends this fall, but you're both going to have to do more around the house now that Mrs. Burns is going."

My grandfather had often complained to my mother that Mrs. Burns spoiled us, that we should do more. I had thought at the time that spoiling was good. I realized too late that it was a criticism. I began to clear the dishes regularly, I asked Mrs. Burns to teach me to iron. I knew if I got better at being responsible, less spoiled, that she would not have to leave me.

The morning she left Mrs. Burns braided my long hair as usual, her eyes a little red. My uncle carried her huge suitcase to the car and I went stoically and dry-eyed to the airport.

That afternoon my mother took me to the town hairdresser and had my braids removed as tears ran down my cheeks. She said, "We will all be too busy now for this foolishness." Her eyes were angry. As the hairdresser cut bangs over my forehead the strands stuck to my wet cheeks. The woman wiped them away kindly. My mother offered her a tip when she was through. The woman replied shortly, "Keep it." My mother was very angry when she got in the car.

Life was very different after Mrs. Burns left. At first I wrote to her regularly, and she wrote back. My mother, who picked up the mail from the post box at the top of our long driveway, reluctantly gave me the first few letters from the West. Our correspondence continued through the next Christmas when quite suddenly her responses dwindled and then stopped entirely. I continued to write for a while, and then sadly ceased. The next year I sent her a Christmas card, and the one after that as well. But I never heard of her again, until one day much later when I was away at school my mother casually mentioned her recent death.

In the spring of the year I was twelve, my school break fell on a different week than my brother's. This meant that we could not take a trip together, and my mother and I just stayed home. On the last Friday of my vacation, he was to come home for the weekend. My mother made a lunch appointment with some distant relatives who lived in the town his school was in. She had been planning an obligatory visit to them for the past year, and I think she had a guilty conscience.

They were, my mother explained, "Your grandfather's younger brother and his wife."

My great aunt served roast beef for lunch. I didn't really like it, but eating was becoming a pleasure hard to resist. I seemed to have lost all energy. I didn't want to go outside, or really do anything. I was fat, according to my mother, and I had pointed, ugly breasts, just starting to show. One afternoon shortly before my mother had abruptly announced that we were going shopping for my first bra, saying, "I'm tired of seeing you flop around!"

I had stood in the curtained dressing room in utter misery, naked from the waist. The saleslady fastened the measuring tape around my unruly breasts. My mother stared at me. I tried to look smaller. The saleslady tried to say the right thing. Nothing really fit. The resulting purchase itched, and I was afraid that people would notice the lines it made through my shirts. I was ashamed. I found some big shirts to wear and would button them all the way up to the collar. My mother eventually compelled me to keep the collar open, saying, "It looks so forced."

At this luncheon with strangers my mother chatted with my aunt, her gracious face turned politely in attention. It had been twenty years since this particular constellation of relatives appeared. I had not existed at the last gathering. They seemed to find this a point of great wonder. A lot of time was spent speculating on the exact date of the last sighting. Possibly, my mother suggested, it was at her sister's wedding. No, my aunt corrected, it was at a cousin's funeral.

I admired my mother's skill at this sort of gathering. I listened to her talk, dreading the slight pauses which engendered a sideways look and a question aimed at making me do my share.

"And how are you liking school?" my aunt asked.

I was failing math and could not understand a word of French. The concept of a "verb to be" made my brain seize. I knew what a verb was. The mystery lay in how this verb was going to be something different. There were five choices, some of them men and some women. I had retreated into dumb repetition of the only French I could master. I hoped it translated to, "I don't know." I knew I was stupid as well as fat.

"School is fine," I lied, looking at my mother, who knew the truth, hoping to see if this was one of the acceptable lies. Apparently so, as I received no glance that said, "We will discuss this later."

My great uncle was sitting at the head of the table, not eating anything; and he did not seem compelled to talk with anyone. I envied him, assuming he was very important. He sat laughing to himself, telling what sounded like small jokes which the women ignored. He was balding, like my grandfather, with a fringe of gray and yellow hair over his ears. He wore loose trousers held by a leather belt. His fingertips were also a little yellow. I noticed them as he played with a squat cylinder of glass, racing it across his place setting. Three ice cubes, swirling in the dark yellow liquid, threatened to make it spill on the starched cloth.

I daydreamed about picking up my brother. I wondered whether dessert would be offered. We could not leave for an hour. Dessert was fruit, and did not take very long. The time until we could get Frank stretched out in front of us. Our hostess knew the schedule, and smoothly mastered the timing of the meal like a flight controller. Rising, she offered tea to my mother at the close of the meal.

The old man gained energy as we got up from the table. He marched through the living room, glass in hand, boldly gesturing to one of the prints on the wall. He began talking about art, then about the Civil War. Almost instantly I could see my aunt and mother tire of him. The two women, carrying tea in china cups, settled in chairs flanking the bay window.

Through the window I could see the large lawn. It lay with a little ice and unmelted snow covering what must have been gardens. The sky was low and gray, a little rain beginning. I was thankful, because usually at this moment grownups would order the children to go out for a walk. I wished that my brother was here, that we had been able to pick him up before lunch. We could have shared this responsibility. The conversation of adults is the work of children.

The seated women clearly found my uncle's pontificating wearisome. Unappreciated, he turned to me and asked if I wanted to see some Indian artifacts. I was interested in Indians, and thought that anything was better than listening to the ladies. Besides, there was no way to refuse such a direct suggestion from an adult. His study was down the hall. In it were several glass-fronted cabinets. He told me to wait, and took a side trip into the kitchen.

The cabinets held only a few items. There was a stuffed otter with glass eyes and what looked like a plastic nose. The whiskers were missing. My uncle returned, his glass refilled. He directed my attention to the other cabinet. In it was a headdress. He opened the doors and took it out, handling it with care and excitement.

"Do you want to put it on?" he asked.

I nodded, feeling suddenly happier.

He gently reached behind my head to place it on me. The feathers fell in a cascade. It was surprisingly heavy, smelling only a little of age and dust. It was like being in a cave.

As I looked out he smiled at me and said, "You are so beautiful. You look like a princess."

I laughed, not knowing what to do with his compliment, and said nothing. It was nice.

"Let's go into the living room and show your mother."

We walked down the hall, the feathers rustling. As we reached the door I got embarrassed, regretting having to go into the company again. This was a lot like showing off. My mother looked up and my great aunt looked irritated.

"Show your mother," he said. I stumbled to the middle of the room. Turning around, I caught my mother's glance. It was better that I go.

Clearly my uncle had not gotten this message, because he marched down the hall back to his study, saying conspiratorially, "Let's get the otter."

When we got there he closed the door, and placing his glass on the desk, he asked, "Do you want the pelt?"

The glass was making a little ring on the desk. I saw now that the wood was old. Many cloudy rings of various sizes stained it like Olympic loops.

"Do you want the pelt?" he repeated.

For a moment I thought that he meant to give it to me, and

looked coyly at the ground. His fingers shook a little as he opened the case. He acted excited. The otter was shining in his hands, but he did not give it to me. Instead he placed it near the dripping glass on the desk. His hands empty now, he moved toward me. He wavered a little as he walked, very close now. I could smell the liquid of the glass. He stopped briefly in front of me, his shoes almost touching my feet. His mouth moved.

"Give me a hug," he said.

I didn't move, not understanding what he meant, or what I should do. In the past, the instruction "Give your aunt a kiss" had been a fairly regular part of my life as I timidly approached any number of strangers.

My elderly uncle was standing very close, but still I was shocked when he put his arms around me. I could feel his hands move on my back. Time got very slow. I could hear the clock in the hall ticking. Far away, like a radio in someone else's car, I could hear my mother's voice in conversation.

After pressing me to him, he released his hold. I stood motionless in disbelief. I thought he would move away, but he reached for my face with his yellow hands and turned my chin up. He was not rough. "Give me a kiss," he insisted.

I tried to look at the ground. I knew I was supposed to be polite but I did not know what to say. I felt ashamed that I had let him hug me. I wanted to say no. I wanted to go back to the room with the bay window, back to the ladies and their boring talk. If this was the alternative, then I could be bored.

I felt his hand tighten on my face. His mouth was cold and wet and tasted sourly of the glass as he probed my mouth with his tongue. He was shaking now. Terribly excited.

I wanted to run. I knew I should leave. I stood still, ridiculously poised between fear of him and fear of offending him.

After a moment he let me go. The headdress was coming off, and I started moving toward the door.

"Stop," he said.

I obeyed. He took the feathers and laid them beside the otter.

"Give me another kiss?"

I was suddenly terrified, remembering the feel of his tongue in my mouth, how he smelled. But as he walked toward me I felt frozen. I could feel myself getting smaller; my feet had not moved, but I was farther away, looking out at him.

"Give me another kiss," he intoned, as if it were a question.

My knees were starting to shake, and as he reached for me I felt my back go cold. His whiskers scraped my neck like a cat's tongue. He lifted his right hand to my chest, feeling for my nipples with eager fingers.

With that gesture I snapped back into place. My feet could move again. I was ashamed. If he touched me he would discover how fat I was. His kisses were gruesome, but it was the shame of my ugliness that propelled me through the door.

I walked woodenly down the hall, knowing that he would not follow, to sit silent by my mother's chair waiting for Franklin to be released so that I could be as well.

That night I got a bloody nose. When I awoke in the morning, the pillow was dotted with blood. As I looked at the stains, my vision made a tunnel. I had to run to the bathroom to be sick. I cleaned up carefully, jumping when I heard my mother in the hallway, sitting very quietly until she passed, trembling, overcome by unreasoned fear. I was old enough to know I was crazy; I just could not think why.

11

My second morning in my father's house was peaceful. I took a shower, washed my hair, and let the water run on my shoulders for a long time. The sauna offered a nice place to sit and dry. I found a Styrofoam cup with faint teeth marks; probably my dad had used it to hold water.

One could walk naked in much of the upper floor with no loss of privacy, and I did so, slowly drying. I could not remember the last time I had willingly gone without clothes. Possibly never. Feeling a shade guilty, I got dressed.

My timing was good, for I had not quite finished making a pot of coffee when I heard voices in the yard. I ducked behind the staircase, hidden there by scrap wood leaning on its other side. *Who was visiting?* I did not want to answer the door, but it was possible that other people had keys. They might be able to just walk in. This was not a comforting thought. I stepped out to see who was at the door. By that time they were looking in.

My company consisted of an attractive woman in her early fifties with chestnut-colored hair, and a rather startlingly handsome, blue-eyed man in his mid-twenties. The man looked slightly familiar. The woman stood for a moment in the doorway, still looking at me carefully.

"I think I need to sit down," she said.

The young man took her arm, appearing a little alarmed, and deposited her in Lew's chair, where she promptly began to cry. I was horrified. Thinking of Paula the day before, I fairly ran into the kitchen in search of paper napkins. While rustling around on the counter, I managed to knock over my newly-poured cup of coffee on the combined surfaces of the floor and my right foot.

I am not sure what the woman thought of my thrusting a handful of wrinkled napkins under her grief-stricken nose, but she took them, wiped her eyes, and began to talk.

"Thank you. I am so sorry. I knew this was going to be difficult. I was so fond of your father, and when you came to the door it was such a shock. Your eyes are exactly like his. Nobody has that shade of blue. I'm so sorry."

There was nothing for me to say, and I looked at the man helplessly. He smiled at me, but before he could say anything the woman continued.

"I'm Carol, and this is my son, Patrick. My husband employed Lew as a carpenter after he left the resort. Lew was with us over ten years. Patrick worked with him on the crew for several summers, when your father was still able to do part-time."

I still didn't know what to say, and she went on.

"I heard you got in yesterday. Really, what we wanted to do was to drop in and see how you're doing. What a shame about your father. We're so sorry. He was such a wonderful man."

Barely stopping for a breath, she continued, "You and Patrick go to the same school. He's home on break now as well." She met his glance apologetically, knowing she was talking for him, but seemingly unable to stop. It was all fine with me because I wasn't sure I could have blurted out a word just then if my life had depended on it.

She seemed to collect herself rather suddenly and exclaimed: "You can't be staying here by yourself! Where is your family?" I didn't answer and she went on, "This is no place for a young woman alone. Particularly after a death."

I could respond to this, and said truthfully, "I like it here. I don't mind being alone."

She looked at the debris stacked around the room worriedly. From this I gathered that she might be concerned not about intruders, but about hygiene. Or perhaps she had ventured upstairs sometime in the past. I didn't know. Lew's reading habits were not subtle.

Presently, Carol started to tear up again; her face got pinker and her eyes wetter. Patrick salvaged one of the napkins trying to camouflage itself in the heaps of trash and handed it to her. She blew her nose and asked, "Can you come have dinner with us tonight? I'd like to talk with you. Wili, my husband, will be there. He'll want to meet you."

I told her cordially, "I haven't driven around here yet." I was preparing to decline the invitation.

She broke in and fairly shouted, "You're not driving Lew's car, are you!" As if it were going to blow up at any moment.

"I haven't yet, just moved it," I admitted.

"Patrick will come and get you." She said this with some finality, meeting his eyes firmly.

He smiled at her and then at me and said, "Of course."

So it was settled. The Patrick taxi would arrive at seven and would deliver me home at my whim.

They left, he backing the Jeep station wagon expertly past the Dumpster and negotiating neatly around Lew's maligned Subaru, now lightly covered with a dusting of new snow.

"Lew!" I said, semi-loudly, and, laughing at myself, poured another cup of coffee. Then I went upstairs to change my socks.

12

The evenings after Mrs. Burns left were even more than usually filled with telephone calls from my grandfather. My mother was extremely irritable and preoccupied. She did not cook, but shopped twice a month, stocking up on TV dinners.

One Friday afternoon on the way home from his school, my brother and I accompanied her to the grocery store, he in the front seat, I in the back. He began randomly changing the radio station.

"Don't do that," my mother warned. He continued fussing, as if he didn't hear her. I began to get nervous.

My mother checked in the rearview mirror and slammed on the brakes. She grabbed my brother's shirt. "Are you listening to me?"

He was confused. His hand dropped from the controls. Then he became angry, even with her still holding him by the shirt.

"What's the big deal?" he said.

"When I ask you to do something," my mother yelled, "I mean for you to do it!"

He was silent, sullen, refusing to meet her eyes.

"You hear me?"

I made myself small in the back seat, but it was too late. My mother turned on me, her face purple.

"And you! You are the laziest white girl on the face of the planet! What have you done to justify your existence today?"

"Nothing. I'm sorry," I said, looking down at my feet.

The car was off to the side of the road. "You two get out," she yelled.

We looked at each other, then at her.

"You want me to leave you here?"

I looked out the window to the side of the road. There was just a treed bank, nothing else. I was shaking, starting to cry. My brother, sitting stonefaced, showed no fear.

When we did not get out, my mother relented. She went into the grocery store by herself, leaving us with the instruction: "Think about it."

A man parked in a truck nearby kept watching us. My grandfather had told us to be careful of kidnappers, that they targeted children alone in cars. I wondered what they thought of children by the side of the road. I was the biggest coward in the world. I could not even look at my brother, who sat stoically in the front seat. I began making little involuntary noises; I locked the doors and slid down behind the seat, waiting for my mother to return.

During that year my brother and I walked on eggshells in the house, remembering to do the dishes and make our beds. My mother viewed this with approval. We ate dinner by ourselves in front of the TV while my mother talked with my grandfather on the phone.

Large manila envelopes arrived regularly by mail. I asked my mother what they were.

"Legal documents," she said, sourly. "Do your homework."

One evening in the spring my grandfather hosted a large party with all the family present. After dinner he stood by the fireplace with glass raised and toasted my mother and uncle's new partnership in the farm. My uncle smiled, standing with my mother. His wife, now huge with child again, sat on the side and talked with her friends.

I asked my mother later what a partnership was.

"Two people owning a business together."

"How do you know who owns what?"

"It's not like that. It's done with percentages."

Having no idea what a percentage was, I asked, "How much of it do you own?"

She turned away and I thought she wouldn't answer me, but she finally said, "Forty-nine percent." I still didn't understand, but by the look on her face I knew I should go do my homework.

My mother was not happy with sharing the decisions and operations of the farm with my uncle. She had been lectured on tact and diplomacy by my grandfather, and impressed repeatedly with the idea that she was helping a disabled person. My grandfather, a perfectionist in all matters, was intensely ashamed that he had fathered an imperfect son, plagued since childhood with allergies and epilepsy. He had made it clear to my mother that he thought she was superior to her younger brother. Now it obviously rankled my mother that this "disabled" person actually had been given the deciding hand in what was originally to have been her province.

It was not easy to share the goods my family awarded to the failed.

I became increasingly watchful after the incident with my great uncle and continued to gain weight. This made my mother uncomfortable, possibly because she was under pressure from my grandfather to produce an attractive daughter. I was not grossly fat or misshapen, but neither was I the smiling debutante that they expected. I was a willing student, and their disgust with me was matched by my own self-revulsion.

My mother tried first humiliation, then discipline to make me conform. One evening when my brother and I were home together, I came downstairs ready for bed in my flannel nightgown. I had accidently cut my leg on the razor used to open hay bales. While climbing into the loft, my leg scraped against the place it was wedged for storage. The blade had sliced through my jeans into the side of my calf. It was not a bad wound, though it had bled heavily.

"How is that cut healing?"

I was near my mother's chair. She reached over and lifted my nightgown. I felt like a horse on the crossties, standing reluctantly for the vet. She lifted the gown higher and glanced at my crotch. She got a funny look on her face that I did not recognize.

"You are getting pubic hair."

I glanced at my brother, who looked away in embarrassment. I pushed my nightgown down.

My movement enraged my mother. "You think you're so special! What have you got that nobody else has? Take off your nightgown! Now! Right now!"

I stood miserably still, hoping she would relent. She got up. I could not stand the idea of her getting any closer. I took a step back, panic urging me to dash through the door and out onto the lawn, to the barn. But I didn't budge. I was too afraid of what she would do when she found me.

My brother was up, wanting to help, but unable to do anything to stop her. To lessen my humiliation he walked out of the room.

She let him go, staring at me.

I sat down and pulled the nightgown over my head, clutching it to my middle, hunching over.

"Stay there ten minutes." My mother sat down and watched TV.

13

Having thoroughly stuffed the Dumpster and eaten another can of beets, I was in the middle of tackling my father's massive geranium plant when his lawyer pulled into the driveway. I abandoned my valiantly-resisted effort at pruning. Judy, a small and determined-looking woman, emerged from her car. She shook my hand and looked around the house, eyeing the piles of equipment. "You're making good progress. Lew had a lot of tools, didn't he?"

"Lew seemed to have lots of everything."

She nodded and began clearing a place to lay her paperwork.

The first thing she withdrew from her nylon briefcase was a copy of Lew's will, saying, "This is a very simple document. Beyond the legal boilerplate, he names you as beneficiary to his whole estate, specifically appoints you as his personal representative, and equally specifically writes out any other interested parties."

"Why did he do that?" I asked. "I have a brother, and it would have been fairer to split things."

She thought a moment and then answered, "I am not entirely sure, but I know he considered his will carefully. I can only give you a guess, but I think it had something to do with the other side of your family. And really, he was a bit chauvinistic. He was not used to the idea of women having employment." She laughed at that, noting the irony of Lew's having hired her as his attorney. She said, "Lew felt that your mother's family used their money badly."

Suddenly unsure of her territory, Judy moderated this potentially harsh criticism: "I do not know the exact details of his divorce, but I know he worried about you. I got the impression he was particularly fond of you as a child, and I think it probably wounded him greatly when your mother refused him visiting rights. Remember, the custody laws were quite different then than they are now. Also, there was the matter of child support. That troubled him, and he asked me about it early on. I think sometimes he sent it, but there were other periods when he was honestly flat broke. I don't know what he did."

I didn't answer, thinking about my grandfather's advice to my mother concerning my father's debt.

Judy went on. "Lew apparently had a long period of quite active alcoholism. He was probably not very functional through these. Nevertheless, I think he felt a great deal of guilt about the loss of his children and the failure of his marriage. I didn't know him in that stage, because I met him only seven or eight years ago. But there are a lot of people in this area who did, and I hear he was bereft. I also hear he was quite a handful when he was drunk."

I nodded noncommittally.

"I do know he tried to contact you after he went through treatment. That was after he got the DWI conviction."

I must have looked put off, because she said, just a little defensively, "I was his lawyer, so naturally I knew about this, even after the fact. Anyway, Lew was unable to locate your mother, so he tried to find you through your grandfather. He said the old man wouldn't speak to him, hung up whenever he called. Lew was furious, but also a little paranoid. He told me he thought your grandfather had the windows shot out of one of his cars as a warning. I don't think it was true, but he believed it. Anyway, it did occur in the same time period and that just made him madder. And, as I have said, he could be a bit paranoid."

"It still seems strange to me."

"I know, but I think in the end, Lew wanted to leave you something that would be yours alone. Something that didn't have strings attached. And also, he was a proud man and this way he could get back at your mother's family. I don't know if I'm right. I'm only giving you my impressions. But he talked with me quite a bit over the years because we were neighbors. He was a nice man when I knew him."

I didn't know what to say, finding myself close to tears and trying to look capable at the same time. I changed the subject. "Chuck asked if Lew had a life insurance policy."

Judy replied, "We discussed life insurance when Lew told me he was interested in leaving you something. He was just starting on the house project, and was living in the garage, which was there when he bought the lot. He considered life insurance for a time, but went cold on the idea. Of course a policy of any size for someone his age would have been very expensive. I suspected at the time that he could not afford it."

I could not help but trust Judy. I decided to take her into my confidence.

"Chuck told me yesterday that there is some chance that Lew died of poisoning. They're worried that perhaps he killed himself. Do you think that's possible?"

She didn't answer right away; she knew now why I had asked about the life insurance. Eventually she said sadly, "Even though he was prone to depression, I really don't think Lew would have killed himself, and as I have said, the chances of his trying to commit insurance fraud are slim to none. He was banking on his house all along." She sounded confident, but she looked more worried. I couldn't tell why and it made me nervous.

She seemed to be growing subtly more distressed as we proceeded. This was a change from my other visitors. She started to say something about Medicare and assets, but grew uncomfortable and decided not to pursue it. Instead she cleared her throat and got firmly back to business. She asked to see my official identification, muttering about formalities; she noted my address in Colorado Springs and asked me to sign on the few forms necessary for filing the estate. Then she informed me, "The filing fee is roughly $120, and it has to be paid when we take the paperwork in to the courthouse in Hailey. That's the county seat. I'll get the paperwork done to give you access to Lew's checking account. That way we'll have funds to pay these costs."

I knew she was a bright woman, but I wondered how she could tell I was traveling on credit. I was pretty sure of my mother's reaction to this adventure. It was going to be a long haul.

Judy asked, "Do you know his account number, by chance? It would be on his statements, as well as on the checkbook."

This simple question engendered fifteen minutes of searching through the thick piles of junk mail all over the room. Two measly four-yard Dumpsters were clearly not enough to make a dent in the enormous mess. There was still a lot of it. As a last resort I moved a pile of Skil saws and opened his desk drawers.

No other shelf space in the house was occupied by anything but a piebald assortment of objects, so I was not holding out any great hope, but my clever father fooled me. There, squeezed tightly in neat rows, were bank statements and documents pertaining to the house. They bore a certain family resemblance to the rest of the mixture, but were tamed to some degree. Once I opened the drawers and rifled around a bit, they began to expand ominously over the sides, and I was afraid that, given a chance, they would return to their wild state. I grabbed one recent bank statement and a handful of official-looking documents and shut the drawer. I returned to Judy like a cat with a trophy.

"Here."

She took the offering, looked at the envelope of what turned out to be the title to Lew's blue Subaru, then broke out laughing. I looked over her elbow. Clearly printed in carpenter's pencil was the word "Save." I started to laugh too.

"Thanks, Lew."

He had nearly twenty thousand dollars in his checking account. Judy looked at the "New Balance" line on the statement and did a double-take, saying, "How in the world did he ever accumulate that much capital? Lew only got just over $800 a month from Social Security."

We went back to the desk. His statements showed a gradual rise in his account over the last ten years, reflecting regular social security deposits of $856 per month.

Judy said, "I knew he built the house from scraps, but I didn't know to what extent. He used to bring things home from other people's remodels, or things that came and didn't fit on the job he was working. The garage was here; I told you he lived there for a while at first. The foundation was in when he bought the lot. The last guy went broke, or got a divorce, or something. He told me so. And I knew the trusses for the roof were a mistake from a job over in Pickaboo. People build expensive stuff around here, and they want it to be perfect. But collecting *everything* for the house from other people's cast off construction items, that's amazing. No wonder the house went up so slowly."

I thought, *No wonder he had so many things left over,* but said nothing.

Most of the checks written out of Lew's account were small, eight to ten dollars. Small amounts to the grocery store, slightly larger ones to the hardware store. Many of the drafts were to a place called "The Gold Mine."

I asked Judy, "What is this place, a bar?"

She answered, "The Gold Mine? It's a thrift shop. They have a lot of neat clothes—sometimes wealthy vacationers buy new wardrobes every year. They just donate last year's clothes to charity. The thrift store runs as a benefit to the library. A lot of the local people shop there. You can find a lot of cool stuff."

I knew now where Lew had bought his clothes.

As she was headed to the door for her departure, she asked me, "Has Todd Smith contacted you?"

I failed at first to register this name, so I replied: "No, why should he?"

"He was a great friend of your father's. They were both Easterners, and worked at the resort together from the beginning. Smitty hasn't been well. He has Parkinson's disease. He wants to meet you."

I remembered the name and replied, "I found an article written about Lew by a man call Todd Smith. Is that him?"

She nodded and said, "I hear he's not taking Lew's death very well. Do you think you're up to a visit?"

"I guess so."

"Good, because he'll probably be calling you. I'll get started on these and call you in the next couple of days, okay?"

"Okay," I answered, and walked her to the door.

14

During his nightly interrogations of my mother on the phone, my grandfather occasionally asked to speak to me. I was always desperate to get off the phone. I could hear him smoking, breathing heavily, coughing sometimes. I had been taught manners, but lacked any skill at conversation. The seconds dragged. My inadequate answers to his questions hung in the silence like windless flags. When my monosyllabic responses became too transparent, he complained to my mother.

"Grampa thinks you're rude," she accused. "You should talk with him when he calls."

"But Mummy, I do talk to him, I just don't know what to say!"

"You'd better think of something. There are a lot of grandchildren, and he doesn't have to help support you."

That spring my aunt drove herself to the hospital and was delivered of a second baby. Another girl, whom they named Tiffany. The baby was pink-cheeked, eventually giggly, and probably the best-dressed infant in a town of superbly outfitted children. Her mother shopped compulsively, buying perfectly fitted, sometimes matching outfits for herself and the little girls, who attended all the town functions for children of the upper class.

My uncle and aunt would often take their shining young family to see my grandparents. It seemed now that *their* little girls were the pride of the family, even though the older child seemed suddenly timid, and was having trouble with her potty training. My mother referred to her as a "spoiled whiny little brat." My mother now also clearly disapproved of my aunt, whose sense of style and fashion contrasted violently with her own callused hands and shabby work clothes.

As my mother saw my grandfather's interest in our family slipping, she began to get a trapped look. She had no career, having never been in need of money while her trust was active. Extra cash was not the real issue. She was ambitious, she wanted approval. The stream of funds directed by my grandfather signified his favor. According to him, to be trusted with even small portions of the family fortune was an honor.

With Mrs. Burns gone and the control of the farm in other hands, there was nothing for my mother to hold up to the critical spotlight of success, except her reluctant children. My brother was away at school, and possibly too stubborn to mold to her needs. I was the chosen pawn, and she rapidly decided I needed to do something substantial. She started entering me in horse shows.

I was big for my age, stocky and muscular, my body pathetically out of fashion in the hunter arena where a trim silhouette was mandatory. The ribbons went to the other girls. As I failed, my mother developed a passion for these ribbons. She drove for hours in search of shows where the competition was scant enough for me to wrest ribbons from the unskilled, if trim, competitors. Poor old Buckeye did his best too, but he was not fancy either.

Her conversations with my grandfather were brief when I did not do well, and she became obsessed with my weight. I am sure she thought if only I was thinner, I would win. Her term for all overweight people was "fat slob." I had heard her answering my grandfather on the subject of my size and I found that he, too, found obesity repulsive. I continued to gain weight.

On returning from one equestrian failure, my mother asked slyly, "Are you tired?"

I looked at her unreadable face. I had ridden for several hours. I offered a tentative, "Yes."

"You are not very fit, are you?"

The next week we replayed the same scene, her face hard, watching the traffic.

"Are you tired?"

I lied. "No, not really."

She thought for a moment. "I guess you must not have worked very hard then."

The conversations with my grandfather about the few ribbons from the smaller shows left my mother excited with the prospect of winning in the larger, recognized shows. I was apprehensive. One evening after discussing my weekend results with my grandfather, my mother announced that he had offered to buy me a new horse. She was elated.

That was how the sturdy bay gelding, Trojan, whose photo found its way to my father's house, came briefly into my life.

My grandfather bought Trojan from the master of our fox hunt, who was a friend of his. Trojan was short, technically a pony. He was excitable in the hunt field, and was not working out at his current job. I wasn't intimidated by Trojan's spirited nature. He was pretty, and he had a history. I collected stories about his past life, proud that he should have led the hunt field, hoping I remembered seeing him as the elegant hunt riders rode through our property, dramatically sounding the hunting horn and galloping after the baying hounds.

We took the horse trailer to pick him up. Trojan's groom was at the hunt stable to meet us. "Don't take the halter off," he warned. "He's a bugger to catch, even in the stall, and he can kick like lightning. Be careful."

"Don't worry," my mother replied. "We will keep him in a tie stall, not a box."

The groom shrugged and handed her the lead shank.

Our old barn had several box stalls, or loose stalls as they were called, for the boarding horses, but the family horses always stood tied in a row of smaller, straight stalls. To remove the occupant, one had to walk next to the animal and unfasten the stout chain bolted to the waist-high manger which was open in front to allow feeding without entering the stall. They had no water in these stalls, but were offered a drink in the morning when they were turned out for the day, and again in the evening when they were brought in. When it was hot my mother sometimes gave them water when she checked them at night.

We got Trojan off the trailer and led him into the slot next to Buckeye. He seemed reasonably content, and began to eat. I stayed in the barn for the rest of the day, leaning on the manger, admiring my new prize, patting his nose, talking to him and Buckeye. I hoped he liked me.

Upon being commanded to do so, I wrote my grandfather a thank-you note, dictated by my mother, detailing how much I enjoyed my horse activities and how excited I was about my new horse. From then on, every Wednesday afternoon my mother met me at the bus stop with Trojan in the horse trailer. We participated in the free Pony Club lessons, taught by various volunteer instructors.

My favorite instructor was a woman named Jan, who owned a lovely stable called Hillside Farm. In the milder months Jan volunteered to teach at the Pony Club lessons, and also invited us to an occasional Saturday morning lecture on stable management. In return we were allowed to clean the stalls, and the older children got to brush some of the tall occupants. The barn was orderly and efficient, influenced by its owner's many visits to the great barns of Europe.

Jan considered New England unsuitable for training in the winter. At the start of chilly weather two huge vans arrived. The sport horses, legs in tidy white flannel bandages, were led up the ramps. The doors were clamped shut and the horses departed in a mist of diesel smoke to parts south, Jan with them. I was bereft when she left, and moped around for weeks.

When she returned in the spring I begged my mother for lessons again. After consulting my grandfather, my mother called and asked for a weekly private. Jan graciously said she would teach me when she had time, or ask one of her working students to assist me in the basics.

I was still hopelessly proud of Trojan even though he was temperamental, always convinced that his last unsuccessful job was better than the current one. I loved to jump, but Jan said, "All jumpers must train in dressage if they are to improve." Dressage, from what I could see, was trotting and cantering in endless rhythmic circles.

I was perfectly desperate to please her, and listened carefully to the largely incomprehensible advice. "Shape the horse's neck with your hands, support him with your legs, then give him room to move. You must balance yourself, and he must balance himself. If he makes a mistake, shape him again, but don't hold him in position. He must feel he has some freedom, to go correctly."

Jan eventually assigned one of her working students to work me for hours on a horse—riding in constant circles on a line until I could ride any gait without stirrups or reins. She insisted that Trojan was unsuitable for this activity. My borrowed school horse was well trained, even-gaited and even-tempered, patient with my bouncing and clutching. I had been depending more than I thought on the horse's mouth for my own balance, but eventually I mastered the task.

Jan looked over the fence one day as I rode, cantering on the line with my fingers linked behind my head. "Good job," she shouted, approving of my emerging skill, "now you'll be able to give your hand when *you* want to!" She then allowed me back on Trojan and patiently suffered through my partner's head-tossing, sidestepping, tail-swishing behavior, saying only: "Not to worry, go forward, try again." She was on my side. I knew this for certain when my mother complained to her about my weight. Jan said only, "It's good that she tries so hard."

Trojan was a slow student at first, not understanding the technicalities of dressage training any better than I. He could not see why he should do endless transitions on command from one gait to the other, or go in straight lines and halt promptly when asked. He was always looking for a jump, hoping for a gallop. Eventually he relented and began to respond to my subtler commands, shaping himself under me and listening. I took him to the Pony Club show that season, and concentrating hard, won a few coveted ribbons. My mother was happy; she called my grandfather and hung the ribbons in our entry. It was from that show that she had the photo of me jumping copied for a Christmas card.

Trojan's previous groom had told the truth: he had a vicious cow kick. One evening I pinched him with the girth by accident, and he struck forward with a hind foot, connecting with me on the thigh and knocking me down in the corner of the grooming area. I lay there shocked, tears running down my cheeks. The kick truly hurt, but I was more devastated that he would do this to me. He was supposed to be my friend. The horse was snorting, waiting for a reprimand. I calmed him down and put him away, choosing not tell anyone of the incident. I had, after all, pinched him.

Several weeks later my mother, instead of taking him out to the trough to offer him an evening drink, entered the narrow tie stall. It was potentially a very dangerous thing to do. As the bucket slopped, Trojan startled. He kicked wildly in the confined space. My mother dropped the bucket and jumped out of the stall. She told me to leave, and did not return from the barn for a long time. The next morning my mother and uncle met me at the barn door. They said there had been an accident with Trojan.

I walked into the barn. A short two-by-four lay cast to one side of Trojan's tie stall. I could hear him snorting, and even Buckeye looked worried. We walked forward in front of the stall. Trojan looked out at us through his stretched nylon halter. One eye was swollen shut, and huge, weeping gashes covered the left side of his face. Blood matted his forelock. As he saw us approach he threw himself backward, almost sitting down, struggling against the rope and pulling side to side with his head.

My mother took a step back and Trojan quieted a little. Dark patches of sweat began to appear on his neck. He tried to turn so that he could see us through his good eye, the white around it showing wide. As he focused on the group my mother moved and he panicked again. The barn was filled with the sound of his hooves skating along the wooden floor in a frantic and desperate attempt to find leverage to free himself. The halter still held. When he quit pulling it loosened slightly, showing the naked and seeping skin underneath. A clear liquid began to leak around the edges, mixing stickily with the blood on his face.

My mother turned to my uncle. "Do you think we should call the vet?" My uncle nodded and they left the barn. My horse stood shaking, but stayed quiet as I reached forward and undid the stout snap that linked his chain to the concrete manger. He took a step back and put his head down while I crawled through the manger to pat him. After a while the vet's truck arrived and the man kindly sedated him and treated the wounds. No one seemed to know exactly how it could have happened.

For the next few days my mother had even more than the usual conversations with my grandfather, but he did not ask to speak to me. I put lotion on Trojan's face as he stood miserably on the crossties. He would not let anyone else touch him. One day the next week as I returned from school the green truck used to haul cattle to the slaughterhouse was leaving the farm. When I went into the barn Trojan's stall was empty. I knew better than to ask questions.

My mother was determined to get me another horse as quickly as possible. The show season was almost upon us. Jan took her aside and said simply, "Good horses make good riders. If you want your daughter to succeed, then you must put her on the right horse." I blushed at such direct support, wondering what my mother would say.

My mother questioned my grandfather about the quality of the horse we should replace Trojan with. His advice was different from Jan's: "We don't want one of the family getting ahead without working for it—she'll turn out like those Jews in that school she goes to." My mother took this to heart. We must win, but we must not appear to be buying success.

My mother remembered my grandfather's advice when she went horse shopping. She acted unimpressed when Jan showed us several nice prospects with hefty price tags. In the end my mother chose a half-thoroughbred, half-Appaloosa gelding. He was five years old, tall, and speckled like a wild bird's egg. He had no hair on his tail, which he carried like a stick straight out behind him in a trot and canter. When he had to ride in the trailer he would lie down and thrash against the walls. My mother solved this by tying him tighter so he could not move his head.

One of Jan's students tried to teach him to jump. In the arena his suspicion and fear of any strange object would make him leap like a gazelle over the obstacles. This fooled my mother into thinking he had talent. Work outside of the arena panicked him. His eyes would become huge as he stared behind every bush, ready to spook if a twig moved. In dressage training he would trot tensely around the arena, searching the sidelines for predators.

Jan was not fooled, and after a brief period in training she had a long talk with my mother behind closed doors; insisting I think that the horse was unsafe. My mother was offended by this criticism of her choice and proud that she had bought the big Appaloosa for so little.

I didn't get any more lessons from Jan after their talk, but I still got to attend Pony Club. The new Pony Club instructor, who had read many books but seldom ventured on a horse, insisted that I ride the speckled gelding with a thick, soft snaffle bit to avoid hurting his mouth. My Appaloosa seized this opportunity to run away with me whenever he felt like it. The instructor looked puzzled as the horse bolted in lessons and said, "Perhaps he is frightened of your whip." She recommended that I not carry one, watching curiously as the horse galloped wildly forward and at the last moment slammed on the brakes in front of jumps, snorting with suspicion.

I was eliminated in every show I entered, yet remained on the Pony Club team because their competitions included a dressage test, a section on stable management, and a written test as well as jumping trials. The team could count on me for perfect scores on the bookwork, and thanks to Jan, I always led in dressage.

My mother was discouraged that winter. She temporarily retired the Appaloosa to a stall and looked for another horse. Having taken a stand against fancy horses, she frequented the killer sale where unfortunate horses were auctioned, many of them purchased for meat by smiling men in cowboy boots. She bought a gray mare for me to ride. The mare was soft-eyed and sweet, but after a few months' work she turned up desperately lame.

My mother took her back to the sale, returning with another project: a pretty chestnut whose testicles had never descended, and had thus escaped gelding. He bit everyone on the place, savaged the other horses, and tried to kick down the walls of his stall. My mother replaced him with a bay gelding who threw himself over backward when the rider tried to touch the reins in the canter. I was never more thankful for my longe lessons without reins than when on him.

I came to dread the pathetic hijacks from the killers that came out of our trailer. My mother tirelessly rolled the dice, convinced that she was saving money. After a while my runaway mount, the Appaloosa, seemed easy, and I settled on him.

The next November I was scheduled to ride in a clinic with a famous Australian event rider. After the dressage lesson we went out on the nearly frozen cross-country course. Naturally, my mount refused to jump again and again.

Finally the Australian pulled me aside. "You would go to war without your weapons?" He confidently handed me a whip.

I knew I was going to go for a ride, but took it anyway. The spoiled horse stiffened as he registered the equipment. As I turned him away from my teacher, he bolted, hard-mouthed and out of control. Disregarding anything I had to say, the horse headed toward the open field that lay like clear water ahead of us. I grabbed the skimpy mane and in sudden anger buried my heels in his sides and laid the whip hard behind my leg. I could not stop him, but I knew how to go fast and if that was what he wanted, then he could have it.

The horse ran out of control around the huge field three times. As he began to tire I urged him on, still furious that he would try to blackmail me and shirk his job. I had lost my fear, and for the first time in my life, gained anger as a friend. When I finally allowed the panting horse to stop, the famous Australian smiled at me and said, "I think you're a rider. What's your name again?"

My mother got out her calendar, counted out another series of competitions and put the entry forms in the mail.

15

Giving Lew's tools a new home in the garage took longer than I'd expected because of the snow.

I had decided that, having been inventoried for his lawyer, Lew's construction materials needed relocation. I'd need help to move the two table saws, but the rest was fair game. First a path had to be cleared through the deep snow. I shoveled one just wide enough for the metal wheelbarrow to pass. After many loaded trips back and forth, my shoulders aching, the wheelbarrow's tire went flat.

I was getting a sense of where Lew kept things in the tremendous surplus. I found a pair of vicegrips and several screwdrivers and knelt down in the snow to remove the tire from the upended wheelbarrow. I could see what I needed to do: just unscrew the two plates that held the axle to the frame, pull the wheel, and slide the axle out. I applied my tools.

I saw that one of the cast brackets had broken and been remade of hammered sheet metal, doubled over with new holes drilled. Lew apparently had used this wheelbarrow a lot. I thought of the stucco house, and realized how the bracket had broken. Stucco is largely sand. Lew had worn out the bracket with endless loads. That was a lot of work for an old man.

I was rubbing dirt from my hands with snow when I heard the phone ring.

"Is this Lew Pierce's house?" the caller asked in a quavering voice.

"Yes," I answered, "I'm his daughter."

"This is Todd Smith. Your father was a great friend of mine. I am so sorry to hear of his death."

"Thank you."

The man's unsteady voice utterly disarmed me, and I amazed myself by asking, "Please, would you come over sometime? There are so many things I don't know about. I need someone to help who knew my dad." This sounded too pathetic. I was embarrassed. I added quickly, "There are a lot of pictures—do you think you can tell me who they're of?"

"I'd have to see them before I could say, but probably I could help."

"When could you come?"

"How about right now?" He asked for directions.

After he hung up, I wondered—how long from "now" was "right now"? Also, if they had been such good friends, why had Todd Smith never been to Lew's house? But then there was the bathroom: maybe my dad had been sensitive about his housekeeping.

I vacuumed the thickest dust from Lew's table and had finished washing the rings before I heard a car in the driveway. I guessed "right now" really meant "right now."

I put my cleaning things away and went to the door. There was yet another jeep sitting in the drive. A man in his thirties was already out of the driver's seat. He opened the passenger door and offered a walker to the very tall and frail-looking passenger. I had heard of Parkinson's disease, knew it was neurological and eventually fatal, but had never known any one stricken by it. The tall man looked as though he might collapse at any moment. I went out to help, managing only to flutter around the edges of a precise and practiced routine.

The younger man, concentrating firmly on his job, acknowledged me with a brief nod and continued talking to the older man.

"Take it easy, Mr. Smith, just small steps."

We negotiated the low step into Lew's house with little difficulty. Then we headed toward his chair, which waited ready for the old man.

He settled himself and politely dismissed his helper, saying slowly, "I'll call you at the shop when you can come and get me again."

"Right, Mr. Smith." The younger man left.

I pulled up a chair and sat opposite my guest, not feeling nearly as strange as I supposed I should have.

"Are you all right, Mr. Smith?"

He ignored the question and took a long look at me, finally saying, "I know your name, but it has been many years since I saw you last. That was when your mother was still here. You must call me Smitty, as all my friends do."

"Okay."

"Lew created a very open space here."

"He built it himself."

"Yes, he was a carpenter in the later years. How long since you've seen your father?"

"A long time. When my mother took us back East. I never met him again after that. My mother didn't like him much."

Smitty nodded, apparently remembering back to my mother's presence in the valley.

"I should have found him. I didn't know he was sick," I said.

"Lew wouldn't have felt that way, and you mustn't either."

"It's hard not to."

"I know, I feel the same as well."

"I still should have found him before. . ."

"You are a lot like your father. He was generous. But you have to understand that he was also fair. He knew he'd not been a father to you. Loving someone as a baby does not make one a parent. He never expected you to take care of him. He wouldn't have known what to do with it."

"Maybe not, but it is awful that he died here alone."

"Yes. All his friends feel that way. Remember, we were here in town with him. But we can't do anything about that, can we?"

"No."

"It's a shame you couldn't have spent more time with him. He was always so interested in what you were doing. He would have liked to know you; perhaps you would have liked him." The old man smiled.

"But he didn't know me at all."

"He heard stories of you. Lew said he kept track of his children through a mutual friend at first. I think he knew an employee of your mother's. Then there was a period when he lost sight of you. That's when he started drinking pretty heavily and got arrested. But several years ago he got news again. He heard you were in college not too far away."

"Why would he care?"

"You don't have any children, do you?"

"No."

"If you did you'd never ask."

"Maybe not. . . What was my mother like when she was with Lew?"

"Your mother was a strong-minded woman. Their relationship was not peaceful. Lew was proud of her though. He said, in a room full of movie stars at the Lodge, people's heads would turn when she walked in. Lew thought she was the loveliest woman at the resort."

Smitty's body faltered again, overtaken by random movement as his disease asserted its control. After a patient interval, he continued: "Lew was not from a grand family like your mother. His father ran a mill in New Hampshire, one of those depressed areas that stays that way forever. Too far to commute to a job, nothing to do and cold as the dickens in the winter. That was before ski resorts. Back then you skied to where you were going to ski and then walked up the hill and skied down. Then you skied home! Not like today.

"In any case, your mother and Lew were from very different families. You know she met him here on a vacation, don't you?"

I nodded.

"I guess you could call Sun Valley a bait and switch from her point of view—you know, when a salesman shows you something nice and sells you a different product? Staying here as a tourist, is a lot different from living here on the salary of a resort employee.

She wasn't happy. This place looks like a little piece of Europe, but the heart of it is still northern Idaho. It was no place for a woman of her class to raise children."

"Maybe not."

Smitty asked unexpectedly, "Is your mother happy now?"

I thought about that for a moment—like most children, not mindful of the ultimate happiness of the parent.

"I don't know."

"They were different. Lew was in control of himself if he wasn't drinking and was awake. She was on the edge most of the time."

I knew this about my mother, but was not entirely happy having it stated by a stranger. Smitty must have known them well.

"Your mother used to abuse Lew in public something terrible. And he would just stand and take it."

I looked at Smitty sharply. This was not a side of the story I had heard. Smitty saw the look.

"Lew had a problem drinking, we all knew that. Ever since I met him he was like that. I never knew Lew before the war, just when I came out here. He was already working at the resort. His friends in the 10th Mountain say he drank a bit at Camp Hale, but nothing like after Italy."

Smitty stopped again, looking guilty.

"I was working at Macy's in 1944, too young for the war, selling ski equipment in New York City. Lew was in Italy that winter. You know the story of that, don't you?"

"I know he was in the 10th Mountain Division in World War Two, but I don't know much more."

"You should know about this, because it's important. He was decorated: the bronze star. There is a good deal of information at the library here because so many of the division settled here to ski. They are an interesting lot. They saw a lot of action. The Veterans' Hospital down in Boise attracts a lot of them for care, now that they are getting older.

"What is the Vets' Hospital like down there? Did they take good care of my dad?"

"Lew was remarkably healthy, considering he drank like crazy, smoked three packs a day and did everything to the hilt. I don't think he saw too much of the Vets' Hospital until he got sick recently. He told me, the last time I saw him, after Thanksgiving, that he was disappointed in veterans' benefits. He said something about, 'They told us going into the war if we risked our lives they would take care of us forever.' He was really angry that vets who never saw action got the same treatment as he did. I'm not really sure what he meant by that. Lew could be pretty right-wing when the mood struck him.

"Anyway, the only long-term thing Lew complained about was trouble sleeping, nightmares. I know this because we stayed in the resort bunkhouse together when I first got the job in the shop. Even on a good night in the bunkhouse, Lew would wake up screaming, fighting. If he rolled out of bed, you'd better run. It was worse if he'd been drinking. When Lew was drinking he was a terror. And, to tell you the truth, there was no telling when he would be drinking. Dry for months and then a fifth of Scotch in him at ten in the morning and on a tirade. He was not a good drunk."

I nodded in agreement; this was a story familiar to me.

"He was moody, inclined to depression, but he was a kind and generous man, the best friend I could ever want to have."

I didn't know what to say.

"Lew never held it over me that I worked at Macy's while he went to war, or that I stayed in the shop while he was a brilliant skier. He'd come and talk with me when the day was over. Made me feel like one of the group. That's what I loved him for."

His hands were shaking now from more than his disease. I looked up at him and saw a cascade of tears making channels through the geography of his face. In utter misery, I put my hand on his and found myself crying as well, tears running silently. I was jealous of this sick old man who knew my father.

After a while Smitty recovered and put his other hand on mine, patting it slightly. I sat still for a while, hoping for more stories, like a mouse imagining streams of grain spilling on the floor, thinking of gathering them carefully before it was too late. That it was already too late did not come to me just then.

But Smitty remained silent, still close to tears as he remembered his friendship.

I could see them in my mind, still young, Smitty's hands stable before the perpetual aspen quiver took them. I could almost see my dad, leaning on the counter, laughing and talking, standing among the skis as the shop cleared, asking Smitty about the tools he was using, comparing their days. My dad had liked this man, this user of tools. I found I was liking him too.

Smitty spoke again. "I asked Lew once about his ability on skis. We were standing in the shop. Your father said: 'you see, there's a base down there. It's under whatever is on top; You just have to find it.' That's true, for more than just skiing. Being sick has taught me that.

"I never thought I had it too easy, until I got sick," Smitty said, wiping moisture from his mouth with one of the napkins, "but I think now I did. I didn't have to go to the war. I created things, made money. More than the skiers. But I never had to find the base, not till I got sick. It's a blessing in a way. Things shouldn't be too easy." He smiled. "It's bad for the character."

I gave him a cup of tea and he asked me to call his driver.

I hovered around Smitty as his man helped him get ready for departure. I was lonely, wanting him to stay, wanting to go with him, not wanting to be left alone with the growing raw spot of my grief.

An expert in kindness, Smitty turned to me as he was leaving. It was a slow arc, his hands trembling more now with his fatigue, his feet shuffling in tiny steps. He pressed a card into my hand and said, "Call me." It was something of a command. He elaborated, "Call me if you need something. Call me anyway. Seeing you makes me miss him less. You are a blessing. Like God has given us something back."

Then he shuffled out the door, his man at his elbow, not quite touching him, but ready, like a bird dog.

I heard the car door slam, and then the second door. The engine started and I sat down on the floor against the door, possibly in the place my father had chosen to die, and wept.

16

My lonely reverie by the door was terminated eventually by a glance at the clock. I had a dinner engagement. I got up and looked in the mirror. My eyes were red, my cheeks water-marked. Bits of my hair were glued to my face. I looked at my clothes. A sweatshirt, dirty jeans with grimy cuffs. Not a pretty sight. What had Smitty thought? Even worse, what did one wear to dinner in Sun Valley? I decided to look through Lew's things and find out.

Rummaging through my father's copious clothing collection, I happened upon several finely-pleated tuxedo shirts and a box of dusty jewelry. There were at least three sets of studs for the formal shirts, as well as a very ornate set of women's clip-on earrings. I didn't think he had worn these, but it gave me a clue about what sort of gatherings he liked to attend, and with whom. I would definitely not have been fast enough company for my dad.

The dress shirts were encased in slightly yellowed plastic from an ancient dry cleaning. I carted them upstairs and hung them near the shower. Finding a clean pair of jeans, I laid them out hurriedly. I twisted my hair in an untidy knot as I showered, but after I had dried myself, I carefully put it in a French braid, plaiting the long blonde-brown mop into a semi-rehearsed order.

I waited nervously, Lew's scrubbed opal studs tacked bravely to my chest, wisps of freed hair escaping and curling around my ears. I rearranged the now lonely counter-tops, and listened for a car. Finally I commandeered one of Lew's dusty bottles of Scotch, gave it a quick wash and poured half a shot. I had thought to slug it down. One for Lew. But with glass in hand I was confronted with the fact that I really didn't drink. I took a sip and thought to myself as I put it on the counter: *Nice try.*

Presently, I heard a burbling sound that ceased abruptly. A car door slammed. Then a knock came. I was filled with anxiety, but went to open the door. The strange and handsome man of the morning waited outside politely in the snow while I gathered my keys. I walked out and locked the door with shaking hands. Patrick did not seem to notice. He looked just a shade more familiar now, and I wondered if I had seen him at school.

Walking to the car, I coached myself: *This is just a dinner.* That didn't help at all. Then I told myself, *People do this all the time.* Not any better. I settled into watchful silence, wishing fervently that I had drunk Lew's shot of scotch.

Patrick almost undid my quarter-ounce of borrowed courage by opening the car door for me. The only thing that saved me from an inelegant retreat to the house was pride and, admittedly, my interest in the vehicle itself.

Patrick drove a white Volkswagen bug, sporting a modern ski rack, but probably twenty years older than my father's Subaru. There was a bit of rust on the doors, but it was very well kept. Green and gold lights from a new German stereo system glowed in the dashboard. I wondered how it did that with the car off. Clever wiring perhaps, but dangerous for the battery.

Patrick carefully closed my door and walked around to his own side. He folded himself into the driver's seat and adjusted a pair of glasses I had not noticed on the previous trip. Then he turned the key on and listened intently as nothing happened.

I was about to offer the use of the fabled Subaru to my chauffeur, when he handily grasped a screwdriver and small flashlight from the ashtray.

Oh boy, I thought.

He looked sideways at me and asked, "Can you hold the clutch down for me?"

I said yes.

He waited momentarily before asking: "You know where that is, don't you?"

I nodded. *How dumb does this man think I am?*

He got out of the car.

I reached my left foot over the stick shift, straddling the middle of the seats and pressed the left pedal to the floor. *Great,* I thought to myself, hunkering down in the car spread-eagled.

My departed escort had closed the car door, uttering a brief word that sounded like, "Solenoid."

I waited cautiously and then, craning my neck to the right, looked back through the extra mirror installed on the passenger's side. Being careful, of course, to keep the clutch ground to the ancient floor mats, I stared into the snow. Barely visible, shoulders just in front of the right rear tire, I saw my driver stretched out in the snow, his auburn head under the car, arms reaching under the rear engine compartment of the bug. Surprisingly, after a moment the small car burbled to ignition.

Patrick appeared rapidly and somewhat apologetically on the driver's side. He opened the door and said, "Damn thing does that sometimes."

As though I would know what "it" was doing and what had happened to make it quit, or start. I still had my foot on the clutch and looked at him questioningly.

He said, "It's okay, I put it in neutral."

I disentangled myself from the stick shift and dragged my leg somewhat awkwardly back to my own side. My driver jumped in, adjusted the stereo and put the car in reverse, apparently about to repeat this morning's expert traverse around my dad's somewhat cluttered drive, accompanied by Eric Clapton.

I asked, "How did you use the screwdriver?"

He lowered the volume slightly, puzzled but not offended by my interest. He said cautiously, "The screwdriver is to start the car."

That was obvious. I raised my eyebrows and he looked guilty. As he began a more detailed explanation I imagined the kind of girls he hung out with: wealthy blonde ladies in tight metallic ski pants wearing lots of bluish eye shadow and sporting huge breasts.

"The starter motor is a little electric motor next to the main engine. When you turn the key, a piece of the starter called the solenoid pushes the little gear on the starter motor out so it meshes with the flywheel, which is how the starter turns the car's motor over."

He looked at me, wondering if I understood the basic fact of one motor turning the other over. When I didn't look baffled, flirtatious or annoyed, he continued.

"Normally, when you start the car and finish turning the key, the little gear on the starter retracts and disengages the starter motor, so the starter doesn't get turned over at a million RPM and self-destruct. Anyhow, the solenoid is devious, and with a bit of corrosion it doesn't sense the key anymore, so you crawl under the car in front of the rear tire and bridge across two terminals with the screwdriver." He continued, somewhat proudly, "A nice spark and, viola! The car starts."

Well, at this moment the bug was definitely started, humming merrily along. I asked Patrick with some interest, "Do you have to do that always?"

He nodded, but said, "Well, not always, but in a pinch it works great." He thought about that for a bit, while turning left onto the four-lane highway. In the midst of a desperate acceleration he added: "Except for the time my mom was trying to help and forgot to put the car in neutral and then also forgot to push in the clutch. I almost ran over my own head." He turned to me, ignoring the oncoming traffic, and said, "Needless to say, I didn't ask her to help after that."

I was silent and he continued, "I also figured out how to do it without any help—you put it in neutral on a flat spot, and deflect the accelerator cable, which is the same as stepping on the gas. Then you can do it on your own, but it's harder, takes a few tries, 'cause the engine has more weight that way. That's why I asked you to help with the clutch."

We traveled for a few miles up the highway before we came to some blinking lights. Patrick accelerated again and handily veered around a drift the size of a pickup, saying, "My mom has a four-wheel drive, but the bug is great in snow too, as long as it doesn't get too deep."

I was silent and he thoughtfully continued the conversation.

"The engine is in the back, right over the drive wheels, but the car is low, it's got zero clearance for drifts."

I hoped passionately that we were not going to run into any. There was a lull in the conversation, and I asked him bluntly, "Are you the one who told my dad that I was in school in Colorado?"

He looked guilty and said somewhat defensively, "You looked familiar to me. I asked around and found out your name. Actually, I didn't know you, but when I heard your name I decided to ask Lew if he had any relatives in school with me."

"How come he didn't call me?"

"Call you? No way. God, you should have seen his face when I said your name. We were working on the stucco layer of his house. My dad would send the crew over on slow days to give Lew a hand. He liked Lew. Anyway, when I said your name Lew spent half an hour asking what you looked like, what courses you were taking, that kind of thing. I couldn't tell him much. Then he spent the next half hour threatening me with what he would do to me if I ever let on that he knew where you were."

I must have looked worried because Patrick said, "Lew wouldn't really have hurt me, he was just making a point. But he was concerned. He said he didn't have any right to bother you and it might worry you to know he had found you. But that didn't stop him from asking about you every time he saw me for the next three years. I almost had to start making up stories. He was insatiable."

"The made-up ones might have been more interesting than the real thing," I said.

"Don't know," he commented easily, "but time will tell. I'm really sorry about your dad though. He was a nice guy."

"Thanks," I said.

Patrick announced, "I have to stop at the grocery store, Mom needs some things." He pulled in the parking lot and backed into a spot, facing the exit down the hill.

"Okay, I'll wait here?"

"It'll be just a minute."

Patrick seemed like a nice guy, but I was glad to get a break. He walked across the parking lot. The store lights gleamed yellow, shining off the ice layer beneath the snow. The building looked like it was well over twenty years old. I wondered if my mother had shopped here. I imagined her walking out the door. Again, not a comfortable thought.

17

When I was a teenager and she realized she might not utterly control me, my resourceful mother began an assault for command. She created her own dress code. I was shy about my changing body, with its obvious imperfections. I would not wear dresses or shorts. I refused sleeveless shirts even on the hottest days. I gave up swimming. I also gave up field hockey, lacrosse and basketball, because you had to wear shorts in the classes.

My body combined a short torso with long and substantial limbs; I had had difficulty finding clothes. Women's clothes were always several inches too short in the arms and shoulders. This problem persisted into my adulthood, which is why Lew's shirts fit me perfectly. As a teenager, left to myself, I wore men's clothing, sometimes three sizes too big, thinking that anything I could get on fit.

My clothing choices barely conformed to my new school's dress code: they allowed "slacks but not jeans." It was the day of the miniskirt and I envied my anorectic classmates.

One time I got sick and my mother took me to the doctor., who diagnosed strep throat. As a matter of course he asked me to stand on the scales. I complied, with my head hanging. To my mortification he came over and patted my round thigh, saying, "This is your main problem, right there."

One summer, just before school started, my mother accosted me, saying, "You look like a slob. Tuck your shirt in."

I slowly did as she said, but replied, "It looks bad."

She had evidently had enough. She spun me around, her face taut.

"I am sick of fighting with you about your clothes every single day! You are going to wear dresses from now on."

I couldn't believe what I was hearing, and my despair must have showed.

"Don't you go looking at me like that—just wipe that look off your face. Look at me! I'm not going to discuss it with you any further."

So, I was sentenced. I went shopping for the first time alone. Depressed, I hated them all: the clothes, the other girls who could find things that fit, the sales people, the fabrics, the designers. After several hours I found only one dress that I could get on and bear to look at. My mother had dictated that I was to purchase five.

I sat in the fitting room, surrounded by mirrors, reflecting endless views of my inadequate self. I had been trying for the last two years to grow my hair long enough to cover my bottom when I walked. It was very long, but not long enough. My mother hated it, and every now and then would threaten to cut it off. I looked at my round face in the mirror, hid behind my hair, and sobbed.

The saleslady must have heard, and who knows what she thought, but at least she showed the decency to leave me alone. After a period I knew I must give up, for it was close to the time when my mother would arrive. I had failed, and I wondered what the punishment would be.

I walked out of the fitting room and suddenly I was angry, not simply pathetic. I went to the cash register holding my mother's credit card. On the way I passed the rack where my one dress in size fourteen had hung. From the same rack I selected four more dresses. They were identical in every way except for the color. The original was green, the next blue, one brown, one yellow, and finally, in desperation, I took one dark plaid.

My uniformed fashion rebellion did not go unnoticed. My mother seethed as I faithfully wore those dresses every day for the remainder of my sentence, without complaint.

In return for my compliance, my mother suffered daily from a rapidly fermenting teenage anger. My rage was exquisitely concealed, if omnipresent; I was excruciatingly polite to her and would promptly do anything she asked. The rest of the time I would stay in my room, reading. This irritated her, for she was convinced that I should always be doing something, and reading did not count.

My mother stamped into the house one Saturday after working in the barn. I had helped with the morning chores, as that was expected, but had disappeared at the first opportunity. I was reading a novel. She glared at me and demanded, "What have you done to justify your existence today?"

I said hopelessly, "Nothing."

My mother's rage topped the container and she shouted at me, "You're Goddamned right you've done nothing! All you ever do is read and eat. You are the laziest woman on the planet! Now get your butt up off that sofa and. . ." Her voice trailed off.

"And what?"

She couldn't think of anything and retreated, slamming the door angrily.

In return for torturing my mother, I suffered in thousands of indirect ways. She humiliated me in public by making snide remarks about my grades or lack of popularity. The inane assurance that she could not attack me on the issue of my clothing took on huge importance in my mind. Before my mother's decree I had been simply inept at dressing; now I was a martyr.

In the first few weeks of school I was sure everybody would notice my forced march into fashion. I underestimated the absolute self-absorption of teenage girls. It was months before anyone commented. Sitting in the lunch room one day with a group of my classmates, one of the girls I did not know very well said, "You must really like that dress—you wear it all the time."

Offended, I replied, "Not always the same dress. I have a bunch of them in different colors." She looked at me as if I was nuts. I said, "My mom got mad at me and said I had to wear dresses for the whole year."

"What did you do?" she asked interestedly.

This was getting a little out of control. I tried to shorten things up a bit.

"Beats me."

My Italian friend Johanna, who had come to my house several times, broke in: "Her mom is crazy."

I smiled at her in gratitude. Better my mother than me. Now instead of a freak, I was someone with a story.

Odd thing was, I never did learn how to dress like the other girls. In college I lost weight, almost forty pounds the first year, but clothes still didn't fit; I never went shopping for anything but garments to hide myself in.

Sitting in Patrick's Volkswagen, I looked down my chest, seeing Lew's tuxedo shirt and brave row of studs over jeans. I wondered: *Is this going to be okay?* I hadn't a clue.

18

Patrick emerged from the store with a six-pack of beer, a pint of cream, three avocados, and a bottle of tonic water. He got back in the car, which started cooperatively on the first try. He looked pleased, and coasted down the hill to a right turn heading north. He took a hard left at the next light and drove down another hill where a prompt right turn revealed a street decorated with expensive looking houses.

My driver made one sudden, final turn and uphill dash in reverse. This left the bug parked facing out, in front of a flight of well-lighted steps. I exited the car before he could move to open my door, but he seemed not to mind one way or the other, taking the lead and asking, "Want to come in?"

This was clearly a rhetorical question. I was feeling really shy.

Patrick's family home stood in sharp contrast to his battered car. The house was built of massive logs; the front doors opened to a large, slate hallway decked with thick oriental rugs. Patrick opened the door and stepped back while I entered. I held back after walking in, unsure where to go. His mother appeared coming down the few stairs to the landing, and greeted me.

"Come right in. Let me introduce you to Wili—he is desperate to see you."

She lead the way to a vaulted living room, where a balding man sat casually reading a group of blueprints, an iced drink in one hand. He put it down and rose, greeting me in English that was heavily accented with German. He extended his hand for me to shake.

"So you are Luigi's little girl, ja?"

I smiled at him and said, "Not so little, but the rest is true."

He laughed politely and asked me to sit down, telling Patrick, who stood behind me, "Get the lady a drink. Get yourself one too. And then get back here quick."

I turned around. Patrick didn't look at all irritated. He asked me, "What would you like?"

I was trying hard to look relaxed. I said, "Oh, anything is fine."

"Will do," he said and headed for the kitchen where his mother was making interesting noises with pots.

Wili was looking at me closely when I faced him again. "You look a lot like your father. Are you a skier too?"

"Yes, but not like my father."

"That's reasonable." He smiled. "Nobody was."

"Did you ever ski with him?"

"No, I never got the chance, but Patrick did. You'll have to ask him."

"Okay," I said.

Wili elaborated. "Lew came to work for us after his knees started to go. He did a bit of construction on his own sometimes; he always had, even when he was working for the lodge. They didn't pay so good, those folks, for the summer work. A lot of them skiers worked on the side."

"Did he come to work for you right after he was on the ski patrol?"

"Well, he ran the big cats for quite a few years, in the winter, you know, grooming the slopes. You don't know about that?"

"No."

"Lew was really good on the machines. He had sort of a sixth sense about where the ground was. Not that it always worked out, mind you, but the man was generally willing to drive off a cliff if the mood struck him.

"One year they were running the Harriman cup down Exhibition, the ski run off Baldy. The moguls got so tall the skiers couldn't see over them. You know, Exhibition is steep. You could basically fall off it. Too steep to groom with a cat tractor. Nobody could do it. Well, the director had a talk with Lew and they decided to give it a try. You know, take the tops off the moguls so the racers had a chance.

"Lew told the director to ski down about halfway and hold his pole up. So Lew could see the fall line, you understand?"

I nodded.

"So Lew drives up the cat track and gets the machine all lined up at the top. He told me that looking out over the front of the cat he couldn't see the ground, but he revved it up and started over. So he goes down the hill, looking for the guy with the pole hidden in the moguls, taking the tops off with the equipment. About a third of the way down the loose snow starts to slide behind him."

"What happened?"

"Well, this is great, nobody but your dad could have done this. He sees the snow coming behind him, tall as the cat and fast, like it would be down that slope. Lew looks out past the guy with the pole and instead of backing off, he gears the machine up. He keeps speeding up as he comes down the hill, the wall of snow chasing him like an avalanche. It never catches him, he just kept going faster in front of it, like a guy on a surfboard, but with a mountain of snow on his tail. He was the only man who ever rode a cat down Exhibition. And he got away with it too."

I didn't know what to say.

Wili continued, "The guy holding up the ski pole must have got an eyeful, I'll tell you! They said they had to rebuild the engine of the cat because there was no oil on the top pistons. Cause it was pointed straight down the whole way, going as fast as it could go."

I thought about finding the base, what Smitty had said.

Patrick returned and handed me a squat and sweating glass, floating a lime.

"Dad tell you the one about Exhibition? That's a great story. Nobody but your dad could have lived through that."

"Nobody but her dad would ever have tried it!" Wili added.

I took a sip. Gin and tonic. I'd have to take it slowly, particularly as my steady diet of canned beets was not holding up very well under the hard work. I was hungry.

Patrick sat down next to me and handed me the bowl of peanuts from the side table. "Thanks." I took some and held them in my hand, passing the rest on to Wili who poured a generous amount over the lip of the bowl into his palm. I wondered whether I should be offering to help Carol in the kitchen, but the mouse in me had found another leak in the bag and could not bear to move once within sight of the treasure.

"What did Lew do for you, Wili, when he worked with your company?" I asked.

"Oh, you know, anything. He was good at figuring things out. Lately he worked as a finish carpenter. He liked detail work. He was good to have on the crew when he was sober; he could tell a great story at lunch."

"Did he drink a lot?"

"Not on the job usually, and not so much at the end, but in the beginning if he'd had a tough weekend he wasn't right till Tuesday. With Luigi it wasn't just three drinks, it was three bottles! Boy, you didn't want to be in the same bar with him once he got on a tear. He was a handful."

"Oh," I said.

Wili changed the subject.

"I remember one more story the skiers told about Lew. It was down in Utah when they ran the tour for the European racers before the Olympics. In 1961. Was it '61, Patrick?"

Patrick shrugged.

"They had the course set and needed to see if the gates were okay. So they got some of them guys helping to ski down the course.

"Lew was the first one. They took his time and sent the next. That guy was twenty seconds slower. They called back to see if Lew had missed a gate, but he hadn't. They sent the next guy; he was seventeen seconds slower. Well it turned out in the end that Lew's run was two seconds faster than our Swiss guy who won the gold medal! The coach's name was Emile Allias. The Europeans hit all the big U.S. races. Came up here too. When they went back home, Emile gave your dad his skis. They're varnished wood. Have you seen them yet?"

"Not yet. I'll have to keep my eyes out for them."

Wili was laughing, sipping his drink and eating the peanuts. He went on, "I remember the man who won; I was still in Switzerland then and they made a big deal of it when he came home. The next year he won the Olympic downhill. I never thought I'd have a man on my crew who beat the gold medalist."

"Did Lew ever race?"

"Not after the war. He said he didn't like it. And he always thought the other guy deserved to win more than he did. He was funny like that in a lot of ways. He'd get right up to the point of winning and then he'd back off. I don't really understand it."

"It's unusual," I agreed, thinking about my mother.

"A lot of those guys from the war had funny streaks like that. Not the same quirks, you know, they're all a bit different. Not quite like the rest of the crowd. Different. Lew could sure tell stories! Not all of them would. He had a friend that came back from the war with him, someone from his hometown, old guy died last year as well, but he wasn't at the front with Lew. He'd never talk about it. All he'd say was, 'We did some things in the end we weren't proud of.' But your dad would talk. I asked him once how he got so lucky to get through the war when none of his unit made it."

"What did he say?"

"That he was lucky!"

"I guess."

"But he explained some things to me, sitting right over there one Christmas. He told me that during shelling, the guys would get scared when they heard the artillery. They'd hold their breath waiting for the bomb to land. You know, afraid that it was going to hit right on top of them. Most of the time it didn't, but if it was close, the concussion would blow up their lungs and they'd bleed to death. He said you had to empty your lungs right before the bombs hit, then you could make it through."

"Lew was pretty practical," Patrick offered, watching me rather closely.

Carol entered, saying, "Dinner is ready."

We got up to eat, and when dinner was over, we sat in the living room once more, drinking a clear, sweet wine in tiny glasses.

Wili looked at his glass happily and said in German: "Grappa, wie umlaut?"

I asked Patrick, "Do you speak German too?"

"Not like my Hun of a father. I'm a Romance Language major."

His mother added, "Patrick speaks French, Italian and Portuguese. He's working on Russian now."

"Never hurts to hedge your bets."

His father laughed and asked me, "Do you speak any languages?"

"I've got enough trouble with English. But I like to read. I was a Lit major before I went into pre-law."

"So you're going to be a lawyer?" Carol asked.

"I worked for Legal Aid in Colorado Springs this fall, but to tell the truth, I really don't like many of the lawyers I meet in general practice. I don't know if I want to go all the way or not. But it does give me something to say at parties when people ask!"

"Have you met Judy Crawford? She was your father's lawyer."

"Yes, and I do like her. She seems like a really neat person, as well as a good lawyer."

"She is. Is Lew's estate pretty well in order?"

I thought about that for a moment and said, "You know, it really is. With the way he kept his house you'd think he wouldn't be good with the details, but it all seems pretty tight." I didn't want to think too hard about the autopsy and what details we might find out there. I thought it best not to mention it.

Wili broke in, "You know that's funny, I always wondered about that too, because Lew was really good at seeing all the angles.

I think he just didn't care at all about where he was living. But he basically built that place for you, that's what he said anyway. He was perfectly happy in a trailer. But trailers don't appreciate in value at all. It took him forever to build the house because he was always scrounging around to get materials. That was a really good thing for him when he retired.

"You know, we could have just come over and built it for him, the guys would have done it, but it was better that he have a project. He didn't like to be too quiet. Besides, it kept him off the bottle. He'd get depressed with nothing to do."

We talked for a while longer, the conversation turning to politics in the valley. I helped Carol clear the glasses and thanked her for dinner.

"The polenta was wonderful, and it was really nice to get out for a while."

She looked pleased.

"Not at all, we really wanted to get a chance to talk with you. Why don't you get Patrick to help with moving some of the heavy items in Lew's house? If it takes more than that, we could send a crew out."

"I don't think it would need that much," I answered.

"I could come over tomorrow," Patrick said. "But right now, you look like you want to go home."

He was right—I did. With that we took our leave.

Patrick opened my door to the bug, smiling slightly. He settled into the driver's seat, still looking happy.

With his foot on the clutch he said sagely: "Never park facing uphill in a car that might not start." Then he released the hand brake, adding, "Or at the bottom of a hill, for that matter."

I looked on with interest as the bug began to roll gently down the incline, rapidly gathering speed on the hill. He looked at me, still grinning, and popped the clutch. The engine caught, slowing our speed abruptly as he simultaneously added gas, turned on the headlights and enthusiastically scraped the inside of the windshield free of frost. We were off.

As we pulled past Lew's car, in the flat drive of the stucco house, I asked, "Is it really that unsafe?"

"What?"

"The Subaru?"

"Not really."

"What's the matter with it?"

"Not a thing. I've driven with Lew in it a bunch. It works great."

"How come your mom said you had to drive me?"

"My mom's not stupid."

"What?"

"She took one look at you in that house of Lew's and knew you'd need a break. If you thought you could have gone to the grocery store, we never would have seen you again."

"How'd she know that?" I asked, certain it was true.

"She said something about the look in your eyes. I don't know. But remember, we got pretty good at this with your dad."

"I guess so," I said, hunting for Lew's keys, preparing to get out of the car.

"What time do you want me tomorrow?" he asked.

"Tomorrow?"

"Moving tools."

"Oh. You don't have to do that."

"Eleven?"

"Okay."

I got out, grateful that he allowed me to unlock the door by myself and stayed safely in his car, keeping it running. I waved back as he put the bug in reverse and watched him go from the open doorway. They were nice people. They didn't seem to annoy each other. I thought of Wili's good-natured bossiness, and laughed.

19

During my later high school years my grandfather's health began to fail. My mother's status thus became more independent as she finally competed directly with her siblings for her father's attention. She was anxious to support him conspicuously in these crucial final years and spent a lot of time at his house.

Now that my performance was not critical, she released me of the obligation of ribbon-hunting and gave my Appaloosa to the thin and aggressive local jumping trainer. The horse was not so terrified of hunter fences and the wiry woman was ruthless. My mother paid the bills and attended the shows without me, saying, "It's great to watch him win for a change." In the evenings she listened to her father's rasping voice on the phone while filling out more entry forms. *She* had come to like going to horse shows.

While I missed the riding and the contact with the horses, I also felt a tremendous relief. It was as if a magnifying glass had been lifted and I had a chance to move unobserved.

At seventeen, most of the girls in my class were interested in boys. Three or four times a year the prep schools in the area would arrange dances as mixers for their students. These affairs were popular and really the only chance the boarding school girls got to date at all.

The dances were more informal than the dancing classes where the students stood in long lines to be automatically partnered for the lessons. Now the boys had to ask the girls. This was of course a social fiasco for most of the participants. Most of the boys were strangers, and in most cases the music was too loud for conversation, which was probably a blessing.

Like hen quail attracting mates, the girls would giggle and

fluff themselves, hoping to be asked to dance. I had no idea how to flirt; all my attention to men had been aimed at keeping them at arm's length, not attracting them. My own experience aside, my mother permitted no discussion of men without summarily warning me of their dangerous proclivities. From what I could see, she was uncharacteristically on target with this advice.

At one of the dances that year, a fuzzy-haired boy whom I knew by sight asked me to dance. His name was Tony, and he was one of the popular guys. My friends stood as though painted to the walls, enviously staring into the crowded dance floor. In the past when asked to dance I had immediately thanked my partner at the end of the song and gone back to my friends. The acceptance of a second dance was admission of attraction. This time I stayed, not wanting to risk this as the only excitement of the evening. I had been to many dances where I was not asked at all. My shameful failure to attract the opposite sex suddenly had a high number on my list of inadequacies.

He asked the obligatory questions: "What's your name?" and "What classes are you taking?" The encounter was not completely comfortable, but was far from being a disaster. I smiled at him, thinking this might be fun, and he smiled back.

The next music was a slow dance. He looked at me with eyebrows raised. Did I want to dance? I knew for sure this was more fun than sitting with my friends. With a little thrill, I nodded, feeling a wonderful sense that I was perhaps acceptable after all. So we walked together onto the dance floor and he awkwardly took me in his arms. Near the middle of the song he was more comfortable and pulled me closer. I could feel his hips for a moment and his hand on my back.

A familiar chill migrated to the front of my mind. My vision got distant. I told myself, "If only he will just stay still this will be okay." I fell off the music a little, and as I shifted he pulled me closer. I felt like I was freezing. All the noises in the room became sharp and individual. As he nuzzled his softly-bristled skin to my neck, the atmosphere compressed. I knew without any doubt that

I must get away. As his harmless lips touched my cheek I raised my hand and pushed him away. Turning in shame, I fled the hall.

I spent the rest of the dance in one the stalls in the bathroom. My throat hurt, I felt that if I moved I would gag. I waited there, starting at the least noise, holding my breath when the other girls entered the room. I was utterly out of control, with no idea why or how I was going to stop it. In my spare moments I cursed myself for being crazy.

The music ended and the hour of departure arrived. I found my mother's car outside. She asked, "Did anyone ask you to dance?"

"No," I replied. This failure was better than the other failure. "I talked with my friends."

"Oh," she said, with a disappointed air of unrewarded time invested.

I made excuses not to go to the other dances.

20

I awoke on the fourth morning at my father's house in time to watch the sun making another pink entrance on the hill. I lay in bed listening to the quiet sounds the house made. I was happy. The thought struck me as strange, but I didn't think Lew would mind. It was a delicious sensation, thinking that someone approved of me. Somewhere, still out of sight in my mind, the idea that my dad had loved me was beginning to sink in.

I got up and walked to the bathroom. I looked in the mirror with a mouth full of toothpaste and saw Lew's legacy looking back. There was a faint possibility that I was okay. I pulled my hair back in a ponytail. I could see why they said I looked like him. Then I went to find something for breakfast.

This morning's entree was canned beef stew. I planned to go grocery shopping later for fresh food. Lew had enough canned goods for a battalion. Most of them were now neatly stacked by category on his shelves. I realized with a strange pride that Lew's house was the first major project that had really been mine. I wiggled my feet in his stuff, rather pleased. But I felt guilty, somewhat sickened, thinking of his body, still waiting in limbo while the formalities were worked out. I didn't know where I was going to put his ashes, but I knew I needed to get things settled for him.

My first task of the morning, after starting the dishwasher, was to call Chuck.

He picked up the phone himself after a couple of rings.
"Hello?"
"It's Lew Pierce's daughter."
"Oh, hi. How are you making out?"
"Just fine. I wanted to ask you if we have any more information."

"Well, we do. The substance they found was basically dissolved sleeping pills. Some people who have trouble swallowing capsules put them in liquids. It's hard to tell exactly how much he took. It might be a regular dosage."

"How do we find out?"

"A couple of ways, but the first thing is to get the records from the Vets' Hospital in Boise, which will take a few days. They prescribe medications and then send them by mail to their outpatients. It's cheaper than having them use the local pharmacies. Anything he had a prescription for would be in their records. It would be nice to know what kind of dosage he was on and for how long. Have you found many medications in the house?"

"Some." There was a trash bag filled with them sitting by the bed downstairs.

"I'll need to see them and confirm the prescriptions with the VA records."

"Can I help by driving down to Boise and bringing the file back? Will that speed things up?"

"That would be a big help. I can get them released to you, but you'll have to show identification."

"That's no problem. How long a drive is it?"

"Just under three hours each way."

"Can you tell them I'll be there at three this afternoon?"

"Consider it done."

We both hung up. This was progress. I'd have to get a map.

My project for the morning was to fill the Dumpster. It would not be too long before this stage of the cleanup would be done. The litter of unsorted artifacts was receding, the surviving relics cowered by the cabinets. The daily vacuuming was starting to make an impression. I had set all the photos of Lew up on the shelves. They made pleasant company. I thought he'd be pleased.

An hour and a half later I heard a crunch in the driveway and the sound of an engine. I glanced at one of Lew's six watches and saw it was 10:15. Patrick was early. That didn't disturb me. I went to the door and opened it without thinking. Standing in the yard was a white haired-man, about my height. Behind him was parked an elderly station wagon with Utah plates. Equipment was piled over the window wells. The man walked with a cane. He approached the door assertively.

"Where's Lew?"

"He's not here." I was suspicious, my back prickling. I stepped out of the door, not wanting to let him in.

"You his latest girl friend? You're too young for the old goat, but he'd fuck anything that moved. Where is he?"

This man was starting to irritate me. I said firmly, "I told you he's not here. What is your name, please?"

This angered my visitor. He exclaimed, "Who the hell do you think you are, anyway, you little slut."

"I'm Lew Pierce's daughter. He's left me in charge of his place. And if you want to stand here another moment, you'll tell me who you are. If you don't, you've got about thirty seconds before I call the police."

The old man frowned and started to raise his cane, but thought better of it.

"I'm Robert Macintosh. Tell your father I came by to chew the fat. And that I think he's spawned a bitch." He walked back to his car, using the cane. As he opened his door he shouted, "Tell that son of a bitch of a father of yours that you're a whore! Who do you think you are, anyway? Bitch." He got in and slammed the door.

I locked the door. *Attractive man*, I thought, while walking toward the bathroom. *Real nice guy. Great vocabulary.* Then I vomited into the toilet. Face down, the last thing I thought was, *Glad I cleaned it real well.*

I had mostly recovered by the time Patrick arrived. We moved the two table saws out to the garage and he took a few more trips with some of the loaded tool boxes. He picked up the flat tire from the wheelbarrow and laid it by the doorway. After he had worked a little while he asked, "You okay? You don't look so good."

I didn't feel nearly as confident as I had earlier. I was regretting my promise to drive the six hours to Boise and back for Lew's medical records. But I wasn't exactly sure how to go about explaining it to Patrick. Telling him "A nasty old man dropped by" didn't quite seem to cover the subject adequately. I was embarrassed by my response, still somewhat shaken.

Patrick appeared to be groping. He asked, "Have you had breakfast?"

I nodded and then shook my head.

"You hung-over?"

"No."

"Come on, out with it! What happened? I'm not moving another blessed box until you tell me what's going on."

With that he sat down on the sofa, looking like he might stay a while. "My father always told the crew: 'Look up stubborn in the dictionary and there you'll see a picture of Lew Pierce.'" Patrick added, "Accompanied by his daughter."

I promptly started to cry.

Over breakfast at a small diner in Hailey, I told Patrick about the man in the driveway. I had left the doors to Lew's house locked, jamming a short piece of lumber in the sliding glass porch door to be safe.

Patrick said, "If you can afford it, you might want to have a security system installed before you go back to school. I can help you arrange it."

"That might be a good idea. Lew's lawyer says I'll have signature on his account within a day or two. How much will it cost?"

"You can get pretty elaborate, but I think a basic one for that size house would go about a thousand."

"Do you think I should?"

"If it was me, I would. I'm sure your neighbor Paula and my mom would look in on things, but you don't want anyone in there you don't know about."

"Who would come?"

"You saw one example this morning! Lew knew a lot of people, and a lot of people are going to hear about his death. I'm not sure who this guy in your yard was, but from what you tell me he hadn't gotten the word yet. Lew had a lot of tools. They're valuable. Have you found the skis yet?"

"I haven't really looked out in the garage for them, just stacked more tools in it."

"They'll turn up."

"Do you think Lew had lots of friends like the man who visited this morning?"

"Yeah, in fact most of his friends were drooling idiots who make a habit of swearing at young women in delicate social situations."

I looked across the table. Patrick was leering crookedly, wetted lips glistening, eyes somewhat crossed.

"Very attractive. Now can you answer me?"

Patrick righted his face.

"We had a man drop by one of the sites a couple of years ago. I didn't notice the plates on the car, but it could have been the same one. A beat-up station wagon. White hair. This guy came out looking for a fight. He said he was in town to have Todd Smith arrested. He called Smitty a 'Jew and a thief.' He said Smitty had stolen all his ideas and made a fortune off them. Then he tried to pick a fight with your dad—as I recall, he said your dad was a fake and a liar."

"I think it's the same guy. Vocabulary matches, but he kept it cleaner for the construction crew."

"That so? Now, you must not have quoted him exactly. Do tell."

I was blushing so hard he relented.

"If it was the same guy, then you know he's a nut case. Lew was pretty mad when he showed up with us. Said the guy had been crazy for as long as he could remember. Was a hanger-on from the 10th. Your dad wondered why he wasn't locked up."

"I wondered the same thing."

"I'll bet, but I don't think you have to worry a lot about that kind of thing. It's just not a smart idea to leave the house without a watchdog of some sort. Just having security signs up would help."

While paying the bill, Patrick asked, "What are you up to for the rest of the day?"

"I've got to drive down to Boise and find the Vets' Hospital. The coroner needs Lew's records and it'll be faster if I pick them up."

"That's a long drive. If you can wait half an hour, I'll go with you."

"Wouldn't that be a lot of trouble?"

"Yeah, it'd be a real pain in the ass."

"Huh?"

"Not at all. I'd love to take a tour of the Vets' hospital. In fact, they say it's the cultural center for all of southern Idaho. It's in all the guidebooks. Please, can't I come along?"

"Okay."

"Great. Do you need anything from the house?"

"No."

"Come on. You and I and the bug are going to Quick Lube. One of the things your dad impressed on me is that it's stupid not to change your oil. I'd do it myself, but it'll be faster this way. It's a long trip down there."

"Is this a date?"

"Absolutely. Finest kind."

So, we got the oil changed.

21

As my grandfather's health faded and my dutiful mother felt more secure, she started sailing on a new tack. She decided that I should be interested in boys. Returning from a visit to the old man, she lectured me regretfully, "Nature is bound to take its course." I was horrified by her prediction that I would fall victim to my inevitable hormones, and allow any sort of unspeakable contact initiated by the opposite sex.

My mother seemed determined to make it so. She complained when I wouldn't let my Uncle John hug me on his fortieth birthday. "Men will not like you if you act like that." I knew it was hopeless to listen to her. And in any case I could not control the panic engendered by the approach of either her or my uncle. By this time I had ceased to let anyone touch me at all.

But my mother was not at all sure how she wanted me to seem. A few weeks after she lectured me on my lack of physical openness, she directed me to carry the laundry downstairs. I was holding the heavy basket in front of me and walking ahead of her. I could hear her breathe as she closed in behind me saying sharply, "Don't do that!"

"What?"

She approached, livid, her leg raised absurdly as she began to kick my thigh. I dropped the basket, trying to get away.

"What?" I repeated.

She would not answer, but continued striking me.

Finally she stopped, panting, and hissed, "Don't you wag your rump at me, you little slut."

Amazed, I said nothing.

"You think you are so Goddamned much better than the rest of us. Answer me when I speak to you."

"What am I supposed to say?"

My mother did not respond immediately. She considered my reply carefully before delivering an efficient backhanded slap to the side of my face.

"Watch your mouth," she said.

I went into my room and shut the door as she went down the stairs. I sat on my bed for a while, wondering what I could have done differently to have avoided this scene. After a while I retreated to my closet and repeatedly bashed myself in the face with my fist. Strangely, I could feel no pain.

The next day, looking in the mirror with disgust, I considered myself the failure. There was still no mark to give the world notice of my mother's behavior. If I had been braver, I could have ended her tantrums, or so I thought.

The fall of my senior year in high school I was accepted on early decision to two good colleges. I chose the one farthest west, a private school in Colorado. It was a good thing because that winter, while most of the other prep-school girls agonized about their choices and options, my family was otherwise occupied, for my grandfather was getting sicker all the time.

My mother was not happy about my college decision, but she had other things on her mind. Several weeks after I told her I wanted to go out West, my mother made an appointment for me to get a medical checkup. She claimed that the forms for college demanded a doctor's signature. I was depressed. It had been years since I had seen a doctor, probably since my vaccinations had been completed by the thigh-patting pediatrician, but I remembered you had to be weighed.

The thought of publicly admitting what I weighed was humiliating. I was fairly sure he would write it down and that my mother would see, opening me up for a new round of criticism. I was sullen the morning I had to go. My mother was silent until we were almost ready to leave; then she informed me that my Aunt Margaret was to drive into the city for the appointment. She made some excuse about not knowing where the office was. I thought she was lying and wondered why she would call on a favor from my aunt, whom she clearly disliked.

The nurse-receptionist greeted my aunt in a familiar manner and we sat down to wait.

My aunt was a little restless, and asked, "Your mother told you about this, didn't she?"

I replied, "Yes." I wondered how my aunt figured I'd known I had an appointment if my mother had not told me. She had made the call in private, told me I was going, and here we were. The receptionist interrupted my thoughts, calling my name.

I followed the slim, white-clad figure into the back, expecting to see a man with stethoscope in hand, but was instead ushered into a room and handed a pastel gown. I was speechless with embarrassment as the nurse told me to put the gown on. It was clear that she meant for me to take my clothes off. I waited for her to leave and then slowly undressed, thinking it was really pretty stupid to go to all this trouble to get weighed and have your blood pressure taken.

The room was cold. I waited uncomfortably in my bare feet for what seemed like a very long time. Then there was a quick knock and the slender nurse reappeared. She escorted me efficiently through the door to what she brightly called "the examination room." She instructed me to sit on the paper-topped table and, after another little wait, the doctor glided in and shook my hand, saying to the nurse, "Let's get started."

The nurse asked me to place my feet in metal holders and amid a sea of white sheets, the doctor expertly separated the open front of the gown and palpated my teenaged breasts, talking informatively about cancer.

I was too shocked to say anything at all, thinking that doctors had certainly changed since my last visit. Then, to complete my amazement, he asked brightly, as he separated my legs, transparently gloved hands ready: "Do you know what form of birth control you are interested in?"

"I don't know!"

He confidently went on, asking his nurse for a group of items on the side table, adjusting his light, lubricating his fingers. He started to slide them inside me, evoking a strange burning sensation. Then suddenly, like a man returning for his keys, he stopped. He quietly asked his nurse for my records, fastened to a clipboard by the door. He draped my legs again and asked me to sit up, which I did with a shamed face.

"Young lady. You are a virgin."

"I know that."

My mother, truly her father's child, wanted no second-generation replay of *her* first trip west. She was apparently taking no chances.

My English aunt escorted me out of the office with a satisfied expression, and I did not have the heart to tell her that I had failed to procure any of the devices I was apparently supposed to want. I avoided my mother, who in any case acted as though all was perfectly normal and did not bring up the subject.

22

Thanks to Patrick's spirited driving style, the trip to Boise actually took just over two and a half hours. Finding the Veterans' Hospital took another half an hour. We arrived on time.

It was located on the hillside to the north of town, looking out over the plains to the south. A life-sized statue of a bronze warrior guarded the entrance; the words "For Those Who Died" were inscribed below him.

The hospital looked a good deal like an Ivy League college campus: a huge expanse of lawn fronted red brick buildings, while several wide granite stairways led gracefully up to them. A second inspection revealed wheelchair accesses added to every level. I guessed it had been built in the twenties.

We walked into the main building, and with a bit of effort located the Social Services department. They tracked down Lew's file, in the custody of a woman who appeared to be on a late lunch break. Patrick and I waited on the steps of the front hall.

Patrick said, "I think Lew was here a bit this fall. I remember he wasn't home when I flew back for Thanksgiving break. That might have been when he found out he had cancer. I'm not sure. Actually, we were all pretty surprised when we heard he had died. Even with the constant smoking, he looked pretty healthy most of the time. Some arthritis I think, you know, he was getting stiffer. But that's not too unusual for someone his age."

"Did he tell anyone he was sick?"

"Not that I know of."

"Why not? You were his friends."

"I can see how he might not have said anything. He might have been embarrassed."

"Do you think the social worker is back yet?"

"Only one way to find out."

We returned to the office area, and this time we were ushered into a cramped office where an enormous woman in a powered wheelchair dwarfed a cluttered desk. She held a slim file on her crowded lap, saying, "I will need to see some form of identification before we proceed."

I showed her my driver's license. She looked as though she would have preferred a birth certificate, and paused long enough to make the silence hang.

I said, "The coroner in Hailey requested I pick up my father's records, but I'd also like to ask you some questions, if that's all right."

"What do you need to know?"

"I'd like to know why my dad didn't seem to be under any treatment, if he had cancer."

She responded defensively, "We can make a diagnosis and recommend treatment, but we cannot force a patient to go through therapy. Besides, Mr. Pierce was treated."

She opened the file and ran her finger down a list on the second page. "He was diagnosed in October. In November he began chemotherapy. He was supposed to come back in December, but he failed to return. We are, of course, disappointed to hear of his death, but there is nothing we can do about that."

"Why didn't my father want to continue?"

"That is a very good question."

"Do you have any insight?" I prodded.

She thought about it for a moment and said, "I have a faint memory of the charge nurse having difficulty with him. He was apparently a difficult patient. There was some issue about his wanting to shower unaccompanied. I gather he struck one of the orderlies who attempted to accompany him in his personal toilette."

Patrick made a small noise of assent, and said, "I could see that."

"Why would he need help in the shower?"

"That is our policy with patients of a certain age and function." She went on, "But there were other issues as well. We deal with a great number of patients here at the Veterans' Hospital. Their ages range from seventeen to almost a hundred. Their military careers have been spread over more than eighty years, twenty administrations.

"As you might imagine, there have been in this time period multiple changes of policy. The current laws dictate that we dovetail our benefits with Federal Government Medicaid programs."

"How would that affect my father?"

"Many of the veterans we serve, particularly those from World War Two, were promised free medical treatment for life. Many of them find it difficult to understand that new laws take the place of old. Because Mr. Pierce was relatively healthy, he may not have been aware of the gradual changes in the benefits due to him. Many of them are not."

I was beginning to understand.

"If my father had become disabled, truly not capable of taking care of himself, how long till his benefits would have expired?"

"Three months is the longest we can keep someone here, outside the Hospice Program."

"How does that work?"

"Hospice? The patient is cared for, but nothing is done to prolong his life unnaturally. For instance in the case of pneumonia, antibiotics would not be administered. It is a very good program for people in the last stages of terminal illness who want to be cared for in the last months of their lives."

"Would my father have been eligible for the Hospice Program?"

"Eventually, yes."

"But this fall?"

"No."

"Why not?"

"He wasn't sick enough yet."

"So he had to go home?"

"He could have stayed, but he would have had to pay for his care, just like anyone else."

"That means the government takes a lien on possessions and subtracts the cost of care from the estate when the patient eventually dies, right?" I knew this story from my work at Legal Aid.

The social worker looked taken aback that I would know this, but she admitted: "Yes, this is true. It is often a problem for the families, who expect to inherit the estate of the deceased."

"The government gets it."

"Right."

"It is possible that my father thought he had given the government enough."

"I wouldn't know about that."

Our interview was at an end. She reached across the desk and handed me my father's file, saying, "Don't lose sight of one important part of your father's decision to remain at home."

"What's that?"

"He was, from the charge nurse's reports, a terrible patient. It is possible he did not much enjoy his visits with us. He might have been angry about the change in benefits, but it is quite possible that did not want to be here anyway."

"Not his kind of hotel?"

"Exactly."

We walked back to the parking lot. The bug was obedient. Patrick and I were both quiet for a while. He broke the silence first.

"I think what the social worker said about him being a difficult patient was true."

"Do you think he wanted more care and wouldn't ask for it because of losing his house?"

"That's tough. He was pretty stubborn. I don't know."

"Neither do I."

"Look, don't worry about it. Lew was a capable man. He'd do what was right."

But I was worried about it.

Patrick dropped me off at the house. I waved goodbye to him, but did not go in, waiting by the open door until he had left.

Lew's ancient Subaru started nicely. I turned south toward Hailey and got to the chapel a few minutes before five. Chuck was still there. He appeared, white-coated, from the back, and washed his hands. He came around the desk and took the offered file.

"Thanks for bringing this."

"No problem."

"Let's have a look." He took the file and opened it on the low table in the receiving room. He thumbed through the pages, checking details and making a few notes. Finally he stopped and put it down.

"I think we can schedule the cremation for tomorrow. We can make a case unofficially. As I expected, your father had several prescriptions running over the top of each other. More than enough to justify the chemical concentrations we discovered in the tissues."

He picked up the file and showed me a name I couldn't read. "This one is a pain medication, quite a high dosage." He pointed to another. "Then sleeping pills. Anti-depressants as well. Your father drank?"

"I don't know if he was drinking recently, but he had in the past."

"Well, I think it's pretty clear that he was taking prescription medications, and I don't think it will be too much of a problem if we record the lab results reflecting that."

"Then we're done?"

"I think so."

It seemed too easy.

Chuck walked me to the door.

23

In the early winter of my senior year in high school, my grandfather's relentless smoking levied its final toll: he died.

In the fall his wheezing voice over the phone had become even fainter, often coalescing into a hacking cough. My grandmother, worried about his generally failing health, nagged him about getting the cough looked into. He procrastinated, bullying his general practitioner and refusing tests. The doctor, finally afraid of the lawsuit his cowardice might engender, referred my grandfather to a specialist. So the cough threaded its way to diagnosis just before Christmas.

"Emphysema," my grandfather said.

"With a just touch of lung cancer," my grandmother volunteered in private.

I went to the library and read up on the subject. It didn't sound good. If the cancer didn't get him quickly, the emphysema might go on for years. Both were unpleasant. The cancer was likely to spread to the brain, in which case seizures were probable.

My grandfather's doctors were in favor of aggressive treatment. Drugs and oxygen for his emphysema, and chemotherapy, and perhaps also radiation, for his cancer. While my grandfather considered this, my family circled the wagons for his illness. In the end, he decided medical treatment would be a Pandora's box of ills: chemotherapy would make him feel sick; oxygen would only prolong his plight. Whatever way he responded, he was bound to die.

My grandfather's embarrassment at having brought the disease upon himself by smoking was acute. Nevertheless, an addict, he continued to smoke. With raw elbows resting on little handmade pillows, his trembling fingers held match after match to each cigarette he struggled to light.

He had a queer little metal tube where he would extinguish partially-smoked cigarettes. The smoke was too precious to be allowed to float off freely through the air when the cigarette was not in use. When the urge soon struck him again, he would re-light the remains. In this way he could gradually smoke down to the filter, cutting his cigarette use in half while leaving his habit unaffected.

We visited him quite regularly at first, then less frequently as his shame increased and his desire for company declined. His speech was littered with long pauses as he calculated his air supply, coughing pathetically. He seemed worried that he had left some details of our lives unfinished.

He became increasingly immobile. His first tactical move was to hire a staff of private nurses, insisting that he would never go to the hospital. When his insurance company balked at paying for a complete private staff, he persisted, selling some stock to finance his demise. He was morbidly sure that, once hospitalized, he would never get out. He could not tolerate the idea that the course of his life would be finally and definitively out of his power.

My grandfather lived only until the evening of my eighteenth birthday. The true cause of his death was starvation. A glance at the future killed his appetite and he began refusing all food around the first of the year. His beleaguered general practitioner supplied prescriptions and advice. The pain medication was taken, the advice ignored.

My grandfather's sickbed was manned twenty-four hours a day by medical personnel who were handcuffed by his refusal to take treatment. At his absolute insistence, the equipment for intravenous feeding lay idle beside his bed. Until the moment he slipped into a coma my grandfather told them all what to do, deciding which procedures he would permit. In late January, my grandmother sitting properly by his side in the room that had housed my brother and me years before, he died.

His sons arranged the funeral. It was a big event; caterers offered a massive spread of food after the interment. His children dressed darkly and stood scattered, eyeing each other while clutching handbags or coffee cups. They met the conversation of strangers dry-eyed. Many men in suits talked to each other enthusiastically after the event.

I donned my dark plaid dress and took a firm-jawed post next to my weeping grandmother, holding her hand and intercepting well-wishers.

I'm not sure exactly when the will was read, but I can't help but feel it was a disappointment for all the children. In the many years they had listened to my grandfather's hypnotic calls, they seemed to have forgotten that my grandmother was the wealthy one.

24

I met Chuck at the mortuary for the drive to Twin Falls at ten. He was ready to go, waiting for me in the now-familiar front office, its computer still silent. We walked out the same door I had entered five days before, but this time he gestured to the white Suburban. As I got in the front, he opened the back door to check the security of the long cardboard box that held my father.

It was surprisingly small. Too narrow, I thought, to hold the man that I had pictured. Apparently satisfied, Chuck got in the driver's side and slammed the door. He sniffed lightly and looked at me apologetically. The air in the Suburban smelled sweet with the doors closed, faintly like formaldehyde with an unmistakable trace of decay. I was thankful for that in a peculiar way. It made it easier to resist the urge to tell Chuck to stop, beg him to take my father and put him back.

Though I was determined to rescue him from what I felt he would consider an undignified state, I had grown accustomed to Lew's being at the mortuary in Hailey. This trip was one more step toward accepting the inevitable that had already occurred. I was a little panicked.

Chuck opened the power windows in back and I did not complain about the cold, trusting his judgment. He had, after all, seen the inside of the box.

"You don't use hearses here?" I asked, trying to get him to talk so I would not have to.

"No, these get better mileage and they're better in snow. We have no crematorium in Hailey; the population isn't big enough to support one, so we go to Twin Falls. We have an agreement with a funeral home down there. It works rather well. They know we're coming, but I should call them in a few minutes and tell them we're on the way. Do you want to stay to witness the cremation?"

"Yes, I'd like to stay."

Then I looked out the window to the south. We were passing through snow-covered farmland. Ahead there was a rise.

Chuck went on helpfully, "The whole process takes a while. Six or seven hours for the body to be fully consumed. No matter what, it will be this afternoon before you can have your father's ashes back, but it's faster if they preheat the crematorium."

I didn't much want to think about that, but I nodded and he took out his cell phone and called down to the crematorium, chatting tactfully about when we would be arriving.

We were passing through a huge expanse of rock that looked like lava. Jagged spars projected upward at random angles, as though a fragile mass had been dropped a great height. After the rock field were more windswept farms, though now the houses were poorer, huddled under bluffs; they'd clearly been built by thrifty settlers.

As we entered Twin Falls, a bridge appeared. I looked down and saw, in a wide ravine hundreds of feet below, the Snake River. The view was familiar. The ragged and mobile banks had changed too slowly for concealment from my memory. I thought, *I've been here before.* Which, of course, I had: peering out of my mother's station wagon driving south many years ago. Remembering it made my throat tighten and I clutched my hands together.

Chuck, noting my distress and missing its cause, said, "Not long now."

After the passing of desperately few stubble-ridden cornfields, Chuck turned on the blinker and slowed. He navigated the rutted driveway of a large white building. It looked a lot like a church in front and a lot like a garage in back. Pulling to the rear of the building, he put the Suburban in reverse and backed up to a set of large doors. We both got out and he rang the bell.

Presently, a round man in clean coveralls pulled up the garage door. He was holding a gurney with his other hand, a tray on wheels. He and Chuck greeted each other professionally. Then they opened the back of the suburban and dexterously maneuvered the box out of the vehicle.

They were extremely careful. That frightened me a bit. I did not want *them* to look worried. I needed all of that for myself.

I wanted them to go slower. I walked ahead toward the brick side of the garage, which housed a massive latched door.

"Is this the crematorium?"

"Yes. Would you like to see?"

"Okay."

He opened the door.

The eight-foot brick room was faintly warm, but not hot. A fine gray dust layered the walls and soot drifted down on the brick platform suspended over the deepest part of the chasm. I could hear the faint rush of a gas flame somewhere below, feel the eddy of air that it created with the door open.

I stood in the way. For a moment or two the men waited, respectfully. Then Chuck asked quietly, "Are you ready?"

And I thought to myself, conversing with Lew as I'd become accustomed to doing: *Ready?* And the answer came back: *Yes.*

But still, I was choking. The grief of a three-year-old clogged my throat as they carefully slid the box through the door and silently made the latches fast. The man with big hands was gone. It would be forever. The aloneness of being in front streamed out behind me, a passed horizon in the mirror. But there was no going back.

The round man turned a dial. I could hear rushing noise as the flames increased. I backed away from the brick-lined door. Chuck put his arm around me, trying to add comfort as my shoulders started to shake. He said, "Lots of memories."

Quietly, I stepped from under his arm, the atmosphere compressing. I let out my breath, waited, and took another. For all the places no one else had been, I said, "Yes."

25

I don't remember much about the drive home from the crematorium. Chuck was quiet, absorbed in his own thoughts, driving carefully, signaling for turns, watching the speed limit.

We both roused ourselves as we entered the perimeter of Hailey. The sky was overcast, concealing the mountains. It was starting to snow

"When can I have my dad's ashes back?"

"Probably tomorrow. They'll have them processed this afternoon, but with the weather starting to close in you're not going to want to go back tonight."

"I can go down tomorrow though?"

"Yes, or I can have them sent up by courier if you'd prefer. You could come by the chapel tomorrow and pick the cannister up."

"And I need to pay you."

"That will be fine. Do you know yet where you want your father's ashes?"

"Well, I might put him back up on the mountain. Do you think that would be okay?"

"That's a good idea, but it will be hard to do with all the skiers on the hill. Are you going to have a memorial service?"

"I've been thinking about that as well. Lew had a lot of friends—it might be nice to get them all together."

"You could do something in the spring if you wanted, let everyone have a chance to plan. There is no rule about when you do these things."

"Spring would be okay?"

"Yes, just pick a date and we'll announce it in the paper when we print his obituary. It has to be in by Wednesday—the paper comes out on Friday every week."

"I'll think about it."

As we got near the middle of town and were approaching the chapel, Chuck said, "Sadie whelped last night, early. Eight puppies. Want to come see them?"

"She wouldn't mind?"

"She's pretty easy-going."

"She's had other litters?"

"Two. Four of her pups are working in the search and rescue squad. It's a good line of shepherds."

"That's why you've got all the maps and equipment in your other truck? Do you go out often?"

"We practice a lot more than we actually have emergencies, but the dogs need to stay tuned. It's interesting, training a rescue dog. You should come out with us sometime."

"I'd like that."

Chuck turned down a dirt side street that eventually curved into a small subdivision. He pulled up to a well-kept suburban house and got out, leading the way to the side door of the garage. I could hear a dog barking—not concerned, but enthusiastic at the sound of his truck. We opened the door and stepped into a heated garage that Chuck had converted to a handsome kennel. A partition of chain link divided it. To the left was an eighteen-inch wooden enclosure with a heat lamp suspended over it. Seeing me, Sadie hopped carefully back inside the railing and I could hear a mewling sound from within.

"Are you sure this is okay?"

"Yes, she'll be fine. She's not a nervous mother, though you're right to ask. You shouldn't bring a lot of people around a new litter."

I could see the puppies now; they were wiggling blindly in a pile under the light as Sadie positioned herself beside them. Though the mother was tan, a rich mahogany and black, all the puppies but one were dark.

"They'll change color as they get older. Shepherds are born dark."

Sadie wagged her tail and looked dreamily at her brood. I saw what Chuck meant. One of the pups was black, with a large saddle of white running diagonally over the shoulders and around the middle.

"What caused that?"

"Infidelity." Chuck laughed. "I bred her to another shepherd in the search and rescue program, but it's possible for a bitch to be bred more than once and have different fathers for the same litter. I'll have the rest blood-typed to make sure, but that's the only suspicious one so far. It's a male and seems pretty healthy."

"Hybrid vigor?"

"I guess!"

"Who do you suspect is the culprit?"

"There's no telling, but with the size and coloring it could be the Pyrenese in the club. We were working the dogs together, but it was days before she was breedable."

"That's what they all say."

Chuck laughed.

"What are you going to do with him?"

"I see an idea fermenting! Do you want him?"

"Yes."

"I can't sell him, and God knows what he'll turn out like in the end. Could be half beagle for all I know."

"Nothing smaller?"

"She has *some* standards."

"I can have him?"

"Sure thing."

"Spring break is in March, would the timing be right then?"

"Just about perfect—that's twelve weeks. Anytime between eight and twelve is okay."

"I could pay you to keep him for me."

"Don't be silly. You're doing me a favor by offering to take him. People don't like un-papered dogs around here. It might have been a problem finding a home. Sadie likes you and I'm sure she'll approve."

Sadie wagged her tail and settled on her side to let her family nurse. My puppy wriggled to a rear teat and began to suckle enthusiastically. The mother lay back, contented. We watched for a while. The pups drank their fill and then reconstructed the puppy-pile. I could see my little male's pinkish-white tummy, distended with milk; his head was buried under a brother or sister's shoulder.

It was a short drive back to the funeral home from Chuck's house. He looked happy, and after a moment I realized I was happy as well. I wondered if that was all right.

"When would it be convenient for you to drop by the office tomorrow? I want you to go over the obituary."

"Ten?"

"Okay. Did you decide to have your father's ashes delivered?"

"Yes, can I have them tomorrow?"

"As long as the weather doesn't really hammer us with snow."

"Okay, I'll be here at ten, and bring the checkbook with me."

"See you then."

I was happy for a while, but I began to feel the shade of depression lurking over me as I got into Lew's Subaru. I drove back through the falling snow, in four-wheel drive, and spent half an hour shoveling his driveway.

Paula's husband, who had been working on the same project across the street, finished clearing their drive. He chugged over the street with a rattling snowblower, motioning to me to step back. In moments he had the drive down to bare ground. Then he stopped the machine and, taking off his gloves, shook my hand.

"Thanks," I said. "That's a really great tool for up here."

"Your dad admired it as well. I'm David. We used to clear the drive for him quite a bit. I was real sorry to hear the news."

"Thank you."

"Will there be a service?"

"In the spring."

"Good idea. Let the snow melt. Do you know what you'll be doing with the house?"

"I'll lock it up till I get back."

"Good for you. If you want, I can keep the drive open for you. I do some snow clearing in the winter when construction is slow."

"Great! I'd be happy to pay you."

"Okay, twenty bucks per hour. The drive is small, so it'll probably only take half an hour. It's a good idea to keep after it in this climate. There are times when you wouldn't be able to get the door open without a path."

"I can see that. Is that why there aren't mailboxes on the streets? How do you get mail?"

"We have a box down in the post office in Hailey, but your dad had one in Ketchum."

"How do you get in?"

"Can I see your keys?"

I gave them to him.

"This should be it."

"The one that says 'United States Post Office' in very small letters?"

"Yup. Take a look at some of his old mail—that should give you the box number."

"I'll do that. Thanks again"

I went in the house. The folks in the neighborhood were forgiving.

I fidgeted around the house for a while and then decided to go to town and get the mail. Maybe do some grocery shopping.

I found the post office, opened the crammed box, and followed the instructions on the plastic card about calling in the back for more.

The infection of clutter had a direct line from the post office to my dad's house. It was a truly magnificent collection of junk mail.

I went to the grocery and moped along the aisles, indecisive, not hungry though I hadn't eaten that day. I remembered the crematorium. I felt like everybody would see how miserable I was, and quickly left the store with only a few items.

I drove home slowly, watching for Lew's street amid the drifts. When I got to the house I saw Patrick's white Volkswagen in the drive, windows foggy. I pulled in the driveway and he emerged, talking.

"I'm fired?"

"What?"

"Give you a car and you disappear. My career possibilities are getting more limited by the day. Cross off chauffeur. Now, of course, the bug is doing its 'I can't hear you!' routine with the solenoid, and I'm stranded in your driveway. Cross off car mechanic."

"Patrick, I'm not sure it's possible to strand you."

"I've been trying to call you all day. I finally gave up and came over."

"Okay."

"Let's go drink some of Lew's Scotch. What is that pile of trash anyway?"

"*This* is a sampling of my father's correspondence."

"Right. Drink Scotch, light fire. Does the woodstove work?"

"Not sure."

"One way to find out."

"Fine. Lew has a good supply of fire extinguishers."

Patrick took the heavy box of mail and held it while I opened the door.

"So, what did you do this morning?"

"I had to go down to Twin Falls."

"What's there?"

"The crematorium."

"I'm sorry! Here I am teasing you and you spent the morning doing that. What a cad. I really apologize. How come you didn't call me?"

"Call you?"

"You know, I could have gone with you."

"I guess I just didn't think about it."

"I'm crushed. But seriously, you shouldn't do that kind of thing by yourself. It's too depressing. Besides, we were all his friends too."

"Like I said, it just didn't occur to me. But actually, it worked out fine. I get to have his ashes back in the morning. I'm going to bring him back here to his house."

"That would be nice, he'd like that. Do you know where you're going to put the ashes?"

"On the shelf?"

"No, I mean after that."

"On the mountain."

"I figured you had that in mind."

Patrick got himself a short glass of Scotch and helped me sort through the mail. I had a soda and sat on the floor in the middle of the stacks.

"You're going to have to write his friends and tell them," Patrick said.

"I've got a pile of addresses. I might have to work on it back at school. I'll do that once I pick a date for the memorial."

"Will your family come out? Do you even have a family? You haven't said a word about them."

"Oh, I've got a family, it's just that my older brother is in Europe and I can't reach him, and my mother wasn't so fond of Lew and she really hates the idea of my being here."

"That's weird."

"That's what I thought too."

"When are you heading back to school?"

"The only seat I could get was on Monday. I don't get in till three-thirty. Have to miss my first day of classes."

"I think they'll understand. I can pick you up at the airport. I'll be doing the trip on Sunday, so I should be in."

"You don't have to do that."

Patrick looked at me with raised eyebrows.

"Okay, that would be nice."

"I promised to take you skiing and tomorrow is the last day. Do you want to go out?"

"I don't have any equipment here, but I'd love to go."

"We can rent skis. When can you get free?"

"I'm going to the chapel around ten."

He nodded. "Right. I'll meet you here at noon. We can get half-day tickets."

"Okay. Do you want help starting the bug?"

"I lied. I was just waiting for you. I think she'll go."

26

I got home from the chapel at eleven-thirty the next day. My father's ashes sat squarely on the passenger's seat, safely contained in a neat brown plastic cannister.

Patrick was early, as usual. His car was in the driveway when I got there, ski rack loaded on one side. I parked Lew's car, picked up the cannister and unlocked the house door, saying to Patrick, "I should give you a key so you don't have to wait outdoors."

"I have a key. Lew gave me one, but I wouldn't use it without you here."

"It would be okay."

"I know, but we need to talk. There are quite a few people out there with keys."

"I wondered about that myself, on one occasion."

I put Lew's ashes on the cabinet he had made.

Patrick said, "I called the security company we use for new construction. Normally they only do emergencies on Saturdays, but they're sending a man out. He'll be here just before noon."

"Should we cancel going skiing?"

"I still want to go skiing, but we should at least get the locks changed before you go back to Colorado. It won't take that long. This guy can talk with you about putting in a monitoring system as well. You can get fire and freeze alarms too, which is a good thing in an unoccupied house."

"I hadn't thought about it."

"I hope you don't think I'm being too forward, but you're getting short on time."

"Thanks, I'm not offended. I've always thought it was a good idea, just been lazy about getting it done."

Patrick snorted and followed me outside. "Did you locate the skis yet?" he asked.

"I thought we were going to rent them."

"No, you goof! The skis that belonged to the famous coach, Allias! The ones he gave to Lew."

"No, I haven't really looked, but I know for a fact they're not in the house. I've handled everything in here at least once."

"Let me see your biceps?"

"No!"

"Could the skis be in the garage?"

"Possibly."

"Could we look?"

I hesitated. "It's pretty scary out there." Nevertheless we headed over.

Even Patrick was somewhat sobered by half an hour in Lew's garage. We found the skis finally, stacked in a closet behind a collection of dry paint cans, a rototiller and half a case of new toilet bowl brushes. There was a small stand of skis, mostly younger in vintage—long by modern standards.

Patrick picked out a varnished set of wooden ones, built with a peculiar second layer of wood through the middle section of the ski. Long leather straps hung down the sides of the bindings.

"These are the ones. Lew told me he used to strap himself to the bindings to make sure he couldn't come loose if he pushed the ski too hard."

We took the wooden racing skis indoors and laid them next to Lew's ashes.

The locksmith appeared. He and Patrick spent an hour discussing electronics while they re-keyed the locks. Finally the locksmith asked me, "Do you want to have the system installed?"

"Do we have time?"

Patrick offered, "I'll bet my mom can come and unlock the house for the installation."

"That would be great."

The locksmith left with an appointment for Tuesday.

"It's odd to think I won't be here next week."

"Let's go rent you some skis and make sure you have at least a little fun." It would have been too weird to say what I was thinking: *I am having fun.*

We drove through town and stopped at a rental store. When I was fitted for skis we secured them on the bug's rack and got in. As we drove up main street I asked, "Patrick, where is Exhibition?"

"The ski run?"

"Yeah."

"Up Baldy, to the left about half-way."

"Can we go there?"

He smiled at me and said, "Let's go to Dollar Mountain for your first trip. I'll take you another time."

I had not skied for several years, but even at my best I was not in the same league as Patrick. He was natural and clever, skiing fast, using economical movements. He waited for me politely at the base of every run, watching me negotiate the terrain and seeming to judge our route based on what he saw. After a couple of runs he said, "You could have handled Bald Mountain. There are some easier runs, but I wouldn't have wanted you down Exhibition today."

"I know, I'm pretty bad."

"No, you ski well enough. But that's different than being confident enough to enjoy a difficult run."

"Riding is like that too."

"You should see me on a horse. You'd laugh your head off."

"I don't think so."

We stopped at the grocery store on the way home and I made dinner at Lew's house for both of us. Before too long Patrick excused himself, saying: "I've got a long drive tomorrow and I should go see what my folks are up to."

"Thanks for today."

"My pleasure. I'll ask my mom about Tuesday with the locksmith. Got a spare key?"

I got him one and he said, "Have a good flight. I'll pick you up at the airport."

"That would be nice."

27

Patrick's now-familiar bug stood at the curb outside the airport in Colorado Springs. It was three-thirty in the afternoon, a clear Colorado day. He had apparently made the trip back from Idaho just fine and was waiting for me, as promised. I walked up to the door and he got out, smiling, "Is that all you've got?"

"That's it." My bag was fuller now, with the addition of two of Lew's sweaters and his urn of ashes. I had been unwilling at the last moment to leave them behind.

"Where are we headed?" Patrick asked.

"Bijou street. Six blocks from school to the south."

"Are you in a hurry?"

"Not really."

"Let's take a drive."

"Okay. Where do you want to go?"

"We can go to the 'Garden of the Gods', if you want."

"Sure."

I looked at him as we drove. His attractive features, now familiar, were less startling. He was concentrating on the road, quickly handling the steering wheel with his knee as he adjusted his glasses and the stereo simultaneously. The "Garden of the Gods" was a spectacular park on the west side of town. I had been there with my geology class. It lay in a small valley, where enormous sandstone monoliths, the rocks often hundreds of feet high, were filled with crags and niches. A path ran the perimeter of the park, stretching several miles, but most people walked among the red rocks themselves. The hike could be very stiff or only mildly exhausting, depending on your route. I wondered what Patrick had in mind.

"How was your trip?" I asked.

"It was pretty long, but I did it in one day, so I've been here since last night. I don't like to waste money on hotels if I don't have to. Nothing about a long drive that too much coffee won't cure."

"Do your parents support you?"

"They pay my tuition, which is great, but my dad is a fanatic about work. They support me by giving me a job. I can make twenty dollars an hour working on the crew. It's not so bad if the weather is decent."

"Do you do mostly carpentry?"

"I do a number of things, some carpentry, but I'm better at wiring and I can weld. I don't like to work while I'm in school, so I make a point of it when I'm on vacation!"

"I'm pretty spoiled, I guess. My mom sends me five hundred per month and I live on that. Sometimes I teach people riding, but that's just pocket money. It's not real steady, particularly if the weather is bad."

"I thought your mom was rich. Five hundred a month isn't a lot to live on. I try to have ten thousand for the year saved by the end of every summer. But this will be my last marathon. I'm graduating this spring. Then I can really go to work."

"What do you want to do?"

"Find a rich woman and be kept."

"Honestly!"

"Honestly? I don't know. I'll have to see when I get there."

"How old are you?"

"Don't know if I should tell you, but I'm twenty-four. A geezer."

"Did you take time off before you went to school?"

"Yes. I really didn't know what I wanted to study and it seemed stupid to find out along the way. Expensive as well. So I spent one year working in France with an accounting firm in Paris, a year welding on an oil rig in Wyoming, and a little time in between working at home and being a ski bum."

"That's why you ski so well?"

"I don't really ski so well, not for my area anyway. It all depends on the company you keep, how good you are. I taught a bit during that time, but it's not something to make a living at these days. During that time I did find out I was interested in languages. And not interested in welding. It's kind of unpleasant. Profitable, but unpleasant."

"I guess so."

We arrived. Patrick parked and threw some coats over my backpack, lying on the back seat.

"Lock your side?"

"Okay."

We set off, Patrick in the lead, at a pace I feared I couldn't sustain. I was breathing hard by the time we got to the first crag of rocks. The snow lay in shadowed drifts to the north of the rocks. Patrick walked ahead, waiting for me when I fell behind, turning to look over the view. Eventually he got tired as well, but by that time I was exhausted. We stood next to a relatively flat rock outcropping, panting. He pulled two bottles out of his coat pockets. He handed me the bigger one silently. It was water. I had a long drink and handed it back to him, feeling better. He took a drink too.

"Want to rest a while?"

"Yes. I'm not so fit as you."

"You're doing fine."

"Right, coach."

Patrick sat down on the still sunny rock. Over the valley in the distance I noticed several other hikers. The whole area would have been packed in summer, I imagined.

"Come sit a moment," said Patrick.

I did so, staying several feet away from him. He handed me the smaller bottle and grinned, saying, "Mood medication."

"What?"

"Scotch."

"Now?"

"It's five o'clock somewhere."

I took a small swig and gave the bottle back to him. He took a drink as well.

"You okay?"

"I think so." I was cold, starting to shiver a bit. The rock face we sat on was slightly gritty; pebbles rolled down the incline as I shifted on the chilly surface. The view was spectacular.

"Cold?" Patrick asked.

"No."

"Liar. Come here." He patted the ground in front of him.

I was scared and hesitated, watching him carefully.

He didn't look annoyed, but was watching me, waiting, seeing what I would do. He repeated: "Come here?" This time it was a question.

I almost asked, *Do I have to?* but thought better of it.

I moved over, not looking at him, and he carefully scooted down the hill, touching my shoulders momentarily while he positioned himself behind me. He handed me the bottle again and said, "This will warm you up," gently holding me to his chest until I stopped shivering. It took a little while.

"You're jumpy! No point being cold."

"No."

It was almost dark by the time we got back to the car, and fully dark when we arrived at Bijou Street in front of my rented house. From the lights in the windows I guessed that Sandra and her boyfriend were home. I felt suddenly shy. I wasn't sure I wanted to introduce Patrick to everybody. It would be awkward. I got out of the car and tipped the seat forward to pick up my backpack. Patrick took off his glasses and got out too, helping me wrestle the pack through the narrow opening.

"Thanks for coming to pick me up."

"Thanks for getting picked up."

"Very funny."

"You're welcome."

"Okay."

"Sweetheart?"

"What!"

"It's a term of endearment. I use it on all the girls whose fathers die and I chauffeur halfway around Idaho."

"Oh."

"You going to be okay?"

I nodded, undone by his sympathy.

Desperate for comfort, I looked down as my chin disobediently quivered. He moved toward me in the dark and I was too flustered to move away. He was bigger than he seemed. As he embraced me, I looked over the outline of his shoulder. I took a breath and rested my chin near his neck for support. I could hear him breathing very softly, feel him make small adjustments in his balance. After a moment he moved away and immediately I missed him. He smiled and leaned down to kiss me. Our teeth clicked together because, very much to my surprise, I was smiling too.

"Let's try that again," said Patrick.

28

Patrick waited by the car while I unlocked the door and went in. As I stood in the hall I heard him close the door, put the bug in gear and start away down the street. I wanted to drop my pack and run down the street after him. I felt as though I might start crying any moment. I told myself, *Don't be stupid. You'll see him again. Get a grip.* Sandra must have heard me come in, because she appeared suddenly in the doorway.

"Well, hello! Where have you been? You were supposed to be home. Your mother has been calling nonstop since we got here. The answering machine got so many ten-second hang-ups it quit working."

"Sorry. I went away unexpectedly."

"You said you'd be here for the whole break. You were supposed to water the plants. They're all dead. What gives?"

"I told you. I had to go away. My father died."

"That's too bad."

"I know, thanks.

"I thought you didn't have a father?""

"I do. Or I did. Whatever."

"What happened?"

"He was sick and he died and they called me."

"How come your mom is in such a fizz?"

"I really don't understand it myself, but a lot has gone on and I'm beat. I need to get ready for my class. Can we talk about it tomorrow?"

"Suit yourself."

The phone rang and she lifted her hands in the air in an *I'm not going to touch it* sort of gesture.

Great.

"Hello?"

"Did someone call for a cab?"

"Patrick!"

"You left your coat in my bug. Do you need it tonight? Or can we get together tomorrow?"

"Tomorrow would be fine."

"The Hub at noon, after class?"

"Okay."

"See you then."

"Thanks."

I went upstairs and was in the middle of a rapidly-cooling shower when Sandra knocked on the bathroom door.

"Your mom is on the phone."

"Fabulous."

"What?"

"I'll be right out."

I picked up the phone and listened to a profound silence.

"Hello?"

"I see you're home finally. Classes started today and you were still gallivanting around."

"The flights were full. Trouble getting a seat."

"From a place you never should have been in the first place. I'm not interested in paying for you to go to that fancy school if you aren't interested in working."

"I do work! It's just that I couldn't get back."

"There is no such thing as couldn't."

"There *is* such a thing as couldn't!"

"Watch your mouth."

"Mummy, I just got in, I'm in the middle of a shower, and to tell you the truth, I'm beat. Plus, it's complicated. Can't we talk about it another time?"

"I'm not interested in another time. If you were listening you'd understand this. I have tried to convince you to put things in priority, but you never seem to listen to me. I'm not sure what I am going to have to do to convince you that you need to keep working at the job at hand. You can't expect me to go on supporting you forever if you are not willing to work at it yourself."

"But Mummy, I do well in school. What is it that you want me to do better?"

"For once in your life I want you to listen to me!"

"I do listen to you!"

"Oh, that's a good one. You listen to me? I don't think so. If you listened to me you would have been at home this week where you belong instead of traipsing all over the western states on some fool's errand that does not fundamentally concern you."

There was no winning this one. I felt my vision grow distant. I looked at the phone and the receiver and it seemed like I was standing on another planet. I put it back to my ear.

"Yes, Mummy, you're right."

"Call me tomorrow."

"Yes."

She hung up.

I walked back up the stairs to the bathroom. The room had cooled. My clothes lay in a soiled heap in the corner. My vision was still funny, as if things were a long way away. I sat down on the edge of the tub and looked at my feet. My legs were starting to get goosebumps, but I couldn't feel them.

I should have shaved my legs, but instead I picked up the safety razor and slowly drew it over the back of my hand. A row of droplets bloomed in double crimson furrows. I traced the razor softly round my thumb and onto my wrist. I cut deeper here, but not too deep. Thick red drops made rivulets down my fingers and landed in the cooling tub. They mixed with the thin shield of water from my shower, the edges feathering and gliding toward the drain.

Thankfully, about the time the razor reached my elbow a thaw began and I started to feel the sting. Then I stopped and put the razor down. Time was still slow, but I was relieved. One of my senses at least was intact.

I looked at my arm. The bleeding was still quick. That was okay. The outside matched the feeling on the inside, and that slim comfort hovered. Not so good, but it was better than no comfort at all. I wrapped my arm in a towel and watched as tiny lights of blood rose to the surface and then subsided. I rinsed out the tub.

When in desperation I had first cut myself, I was afraid people would notice. I worried that they would see the marks and know I was crazy. Then I would be ashamed, so I hid the marks. But it was odd; as with the five identical dresses of my youth, no one was looking.

I went to my bedroom and unpacked my backpack. When my hand came to the brown plastic box, I pulled it out awkwardly, not wanting to start the bleeding again, suddenly ashamed of myself.

I put the cannister on my bookshelf. I stared at it for a while. Then, like a second thaw, I began to cry. Silently, as I had learned to do as a child. I wanted my daddy back, I wanted to go home. Suddenly frightened, I pulled one of the ski sweaters to my chest and hugged it there. I was still, quieting my breathing and listening intently for faint noises through the house. After a while I slept.

29

I went to class the next morning and tried to focus on the tasks at hand. I got a copy of the syllabus the from the instructor, bought my books and started working on what I had missed. My college worked on a block rather than a semester system. Classes ran one at a time, focussed and intensive. You couldn't afford to get behind—a day or two in some classes could make it impossible to catch up.

I worked for an hour in the library after my class. Close to noon I walked across the quad to the student center to meet Patrick. The Hub was a small café. It operated from one side of the food service kitchen that served the on-campus students' cafeteria. They sold a lot of coffee and stale cookies. The cafeteria entrees sat sweltering above steam baths, largely ignored by those free to eat other things.

I sat down, five minutes late, and waited. At quarter past twelve I decided I'd made a mistake and got my things ready to leave. Yesterday seemed pretty far away now. I wondered how I had gotten the energy to sort four Dumpsters full of disorder. I felt flat: a crushed snail, foot departed, shell imploding.

As soon as I walked out of the student center I saw Patrick. He was talking to an attractive woman with nicely styled dark brown hair. She was dressed in high heels and a tight but fashionable suit. After a moment he excused himself and began rapidly walking toward the diner.

Great, this is going to be fun, I told myself. *I'm not up for competition.* I tried to disappear back into the building, wondering where I could hide. He called my name. I was stuck.

"Hey, sorry I'm late. My class went overtime."

"That's okay."

"You mad?"

"I don't think so."

"Let's go someplace else. I actually don't hang out here, it's just the closest place to my class and my professor is enthusiastic about our time. She's Italian and she can talk a blue streak. Hard to follow. Women talk faster than men anyway, and in Italian! You should try to understand. She's just about impossible if you don't have an idea before you get there."

"Is that who you were talking with?"

"Yup, she walked out with me. It's hard to get women in heels to jog, but I tried."

I thought of the woman in the tight suit, imagined her jogging. It seemed funny. I thought to myself, *How stupid can one person get? The guy is fifteen minutes late and it's the end of the world. Get a grip.*

"I'm sorry."

"Honey, you've got this backwards: *I* was the one who was late. I am supposed to apologize to you; you are supposed to hold it over my head and demand to be taken somewhere expensive for lunch, pouting slightly until I make it up to you. My father taught me these things. My mom's good at it—got to be, living with a German. We'll have to talk with your mother, see what she was thinking."

To my utter mortification, right there on the quad I started to cry.

"I'm sorry." I sniffed inelegantly.

"Boy, did I put my foot in it, or what? That wasn't very helpful, was it? Come on. You can tell me in the car. After we eat, that is. Get in."

"Please, Patrick, I don't want to go anywhere. Could you just take me home?"

"Sweetie, my fragile male ego is taking a beating. I finally get to kiss the girl I have been stalking around campus for years, risking arrest to bring back tales of glory to her disenfranchised father.

Then she thinks about the whole thing for twelve hours and all she can say is 'Take me home'? Have a heart!"

"Patrick, it's not going to work."

"You don't like me?"

I was truly crying now. He stopped the car and faced me. I burst out, "I'm lonely whenever you're not with me, I can't wait to see you again, I'm desperate when you leave."

"So, what's the problem?"

"You're about scaring me to death."

"Well, it's a start."

"You are impossible!"

"My mother says that too."

Patrick drove toward the middle of town and parked.

Before we got out of the car he asked me: "Are you really okay? You've been through a lot."

"I think it's okay."

"Right, come on. Let's get something to eat."

We went to a restaurant combined with a bookstore called Poor Richard's Feed and Read. We foraged among the books while waiting for our meal. It took a little while, and after a time we abandoned the distraction and began our class work.

Patrick asked, "What are you studying this block?"

"Historical Essay. It should be interesting—T.K. Barton is teaching it. He's great."

"The guy with the big tongue always hanging out?"

"Uh-huh. Great lecturer. Anyway, the class will be two weeks of research from primary sources and then writing three drafts of a major essay. You know, the first version, rewrite, the second, rewrite and then write it again."

"I'm getting sleepy just thinking about it."

"T.K. is really interesting though. He's got a great sense of humor."

"I think my hot Italian is better-looking."

"Possibly, but only if you're attracted to women."

"No harm in that. What are primary sources?"

"Not books on a general subject, like textbooks. Primary sources are letters, articles or interviews from someone on the scene at the time. The usual places you get them are diplomatic notes and reports from foreign embassies. But the material has to be declassified, and that takes a while. Harder to research recent events."

"Where are they kept?"

"Government repositories. Selected libraries all over the country keep historical documents. The college library is one of them. It's unusual for a school this size."

"That's handy if T.K. says you can't go on secondhand opinions."

"Right. You shouldn't form historical opinions based on someone else's digested sources."

"Good advice. Want me to take you home now?"

"I probably ought to."

"You Easterners are a complicated lot."

Patrick stopped outside my house and rummaged around in the tiny glove compartment for a pen. He located a scrap of paper and wrote down his number, handing it to me.

"You give me a call?"

"You want my number too?"

"I know your number, nut case, I've called you. You're in the book. I'm not. Roommate has the phone. Give me a kiss?"

"Okay."

"That's nice. Hey, what's this? You been playing in concertina wire again?"

Patrick was holding my arm and had glanced down at the top of my hand. I made sure not to turn it over.

"I cut myself." I took my hand away, picked up my coat and opened the car door.

He looked at me sharply, but only said, "You be careful, okay?"

I went inside and found I was alone. The sound of Patrick's receding vehicle didn't bother me this afternoon the way it had the night before. *Improvement*, I thought, quietly rubbing my forearm. It hurt today.

I started to work on the T.K. handouts.

Sandra and Roger returned around four. I heard them talking downstairs, and put down my books. They were in the kitchen, perched on the counters amid a rich collection of dirty dishes.

"Hey, how's it going?"

They both looked at me, closing ranks. Sandra asked, "Did you check the messages?"

"No."

"You're hopeless! Last week it was your mother and your disappearing father, now it's your brother. You don't need a love life, you need a personal secretary. We've got enough drama to keep an opera company occupied."

"Where did he call from?"

"He's back East someplace."

"Not overseas?"

"Beats me, but the line was good and the area code is normal. I saved the message—go listen for yourself."

The recorder hissed, rewinding the tape, and my brother's clear voice came over the machine, responding to Sandra's invitation to leave a message.

"This is Franklin Pierce. I am trying to contact my sister. I can be reached at the following number."

The digits he recited were my mother's phone number in New York state, where my mother had moved after she abandoned her joint venture at the farm with my uncle.

30

My grandfather's unprofitable death had created a ripple in the family universe that dislodged loyalties and created a landslide of conflict between his children. Within weeks of his passing, the siblings began to bicker. Marriages, propped up by the old man, came rapidly to divorce. The partnership he bound most closely, that of my mother and uncle, turned into the battle with the most casualties. My grandmother surveyed the scene and wisely went back to social work, waiting for the tempests to subside.

My mother had a series of truly rancorous arguments with my uncle the fall of my freshman year of college. By Thanksgiving they were not speaking. By Christmas she had begun quietly feeling out her options in other states. Valentine's Day came, and she had bolted her part of the farm shut and left for New York state.

My uncle went from being my mother's project to being her nemesis. She could not bear to speak his name without slur. She would attend no function where he might appear. Eventually, in the coming years, lawyers would arrange the sale of her half of the New England land for far less than it was worth, and after many hours of expensive negotiation.

In my mother's case absence didn't make the heart grow fonder; it made it more bitter. The passage of time only confirmed her hatred of this man she had lived next to for fifteen years, with whom she had shared meals and work on a daily basis. When she moved out she was simply mad. But with each passing month her fruitless anger fermented to a perpetually enraged fury.

Eventually, after renting a series of houses in a small upstate New York town, she settled on a large property with small barn. In order to shelter some of her still-hefty income from tax collectors, she raised a series of unsuccessful racehorses. The logic that she spent one hundred percent to save the thirty percent was eternally lost on her. My mother continued to roll the dice.

My mother had gone on vacation with her sister the fall after she left the farm. That was normal, but this time instead of boarding her two terriers, she had them euthanized. The young dogs were healthy, but she said they barked too much when she left them in the car.

When she got home she wanted a clean start. The next companion was an optimistic and rangy mixed-breed, deaf to all entreaties for obedience, an inveterate trash investigator and livestock chaser. I watched nervously for her next vacation.

31

I wanted to talk with my brother, but the ominous chance of my mother's picking up the phone outweighed my desire. He'd have to call me back. Then I thought, *Lew was his father too, he has a right to know.* Then, *Idiot! of course he knows, he's with Mummy, and you think she'll have kept quiet? Not a chance.* The phone rang, and I watched it suspiciously.

When I heard Sandra moving in the kitchen I picked it up. "Hello?"

"Remember that movie, about the cab driver in New York?"

"Robert Deniro starred?"

"That's it."

"This is not comforting."

"It's on at the student center. Want to go?"

"I've got work to do."

"Me too. How about we both work fast and then go out?"

"All right."

"I'll pick you up at 8:30."

"Okay."

He hung up.

Half an hour before Patrick was due I quit work and hopped in the shower. When Sandra knocked on the door I was sure it was the phone again.

"What?"

"There's this blue-eyed hunk of a male creature, with a body to make you pass out, sitting in our living room, which is a mess, asking to see you, who are butt-naked in the shower."

"Oh."

"Shall I send him up?"

"No!"

"You should tell me when you're expecting company. The place is a wreck." She went back downstairs.

I rinsed the soap off and got out of the shower, wrapping my hair in a towel. In my room I found a clean pair of jeans and dragged them on over my wet skin. I located a bra behind the wastebasket, where it had fallen, and fastened it. I did my best to dry my hair with the towel, and pulled a flannel shirt over my head. The thought of Patrick sitting in our living room chatting with Sandra was not comfortable. I grabbed my socks and running shoes and padded down the stairs.

Patrick looked happy enough, apparently oblivious to the mess. Sandra had found a beer for him, a prized possession in our underage household. He was reading a copy of *Sports Illustrated*, one leg crossed over his thigh to support it. He glanced up when I came in the room and got a funny look on his face. I must have appeared pretty untidy.

"You all set?"

"I think so."

He got up and walked back into the kitchen with the empty bottle. Sandra was in the kitchen, and he must have said something to her because she laughed coquettishly. He appeared again, saying, "Let's go."

The student center was crowded. Patrick saw several people he knew and nodded, politely declining to speak with them. We found seats just as the movie began. I was a little nervous, sitting that long next to him, but he stayed properly on his side. This was not how I had expected dating to be. But then, neither was the Quick Lube in Hailey.

Patrick drove me home and we chatted about the movie.

Again, he politely asked for a kiss and politely received it with a smile. Again, he waited by the car while I unlocked my door and turned to wave.

Sandra met me in the hall, where she was hovering, awaiting my return.

"Your brother called a while ago. He left a different number, but he said he's going to call you early in the morning."

"Thanks."

"Well?"

"Well, what?"

"Who is that guy?"

"His name is Patrick."

"I know that. Where'd you meet him?"

"My dad worked for his father in Sun Valley."

"Sun Valley. That's pretty ritzy."

"It's a nice place."

"Do you think he likes you?"

"I think so."

"Are you two, you know?"

"No."

"When are you going to loosen up?"

"Beats me."

32

I was up early waiting by the phone, drinking coffee and trying to read. I wondered if it was okay to call my brother this early. It was 8 a.m. for him, with the time change. I was about ready to dial when the phone obligingly rang.

"Hello?"

"Hey, Sis?"

"Yeah, it's me."

"How goes it?"

"Okay, I guess. Mummy tell you about Lew?"

"She did nothing if not that. I couldn't wait to get out of there."

"Is she really in a stew?"

"I'll say. My first clue was the calls all over Europe to locate me through credit card charges. The police in Frankfurt about scared me to death asking all over the south side for me: 'Der Amerikaner mit den vielen Haaren.' Not good for business."

I made a point never to ask my brother about his work. He'd been on his own since he was seventeen. I suspected he was trading regularly in a modern version of an ancient family tradition. What kind of drugs he might be dealing was better left a mystery.

When Franklin dropped out of high school our mother quit supporting him instantly. He hadn't missed a beat: simply pierced an ear, bought a backpack and went out on the road. Money never seemed to be a big issue for him. In fact, he'd offered me loans several times when our mother was traveling and forgot to arrange my allowance. I always wondered if he was angry at all the financial support I got from her. If so, he never mentioned it. He seemed happy to see me when we got together, thankful, I think, that I was tactful about my questions.

"Are you okay?" I asked him.

"Fine, just slightly bummed to be back in America. But the food on the flight was good. Mum sent me a prepaid ticket home. The only message I got was that someone had died. That's not the kind of thing you ask questions about from three thousand miles. I got on the plane. Now I hear that it's not the death that's got her knickers in a twist, but the fact that the old codger gave you his house."

"How did she find that out?"

"Opened my mail, damn her. Apparently the law is that everybody mentioned in the will, even if they aren't mentioned fondly, gets to have a copy."

"Oh. I'm sorry."

"I don't want to be in one place anyway, so a house wouldn't suit me, but I could have rented it out."

"I'm not sure it would work for that."

"What I want to know is, why did he glom onto you and not me or both of us?"

"I asked his lawyer that too."

"What did he say?"

"It's a she. She didn't know either."

"Had you even met him?"

"Not since we both had."

"So how come he left it all to you?"

"I really don't know."

"What's it like?"

"Not too big, about five miles south of Ketchum."

"Greek to me. I thought he lived in Sun Valley."

"Sun Valley is the resort. Ketchum and Hailey are the towns."

"Oh. Where is he now?"

"On my desk. I had his body cremated."

"I wish you had asked me. I might have liked to see him buried."

"We could do that still, but it was kind of complicated at the time."

"I guess so. If Mummy could get hold of me, how come you couldn't?"

"I didn't want to call the police."

"Good point."

"I want to have a memorial service. Do you think you can come?"

"Maybe—when is it?"

I told him, and we said goodbye and hung up.

I buried myself in the library for the next two days, and it was Friday before I really came up for air. The phone had been quiet. Sandra and Roger were working or necking or whatever it was that they did in their room. I looked for Patrick after classes, but there was no sign of him.

So when I walked home on Friday and found a message from Patrick on the phone, I was elated. I called him back right away. An unfamiliar male voice answered the phone. There was a peculiar screeching in the background, something like a midget at full volume screaming, "Hola! Hola!"

The man said, "I'll get him," and put the phone down with a clink. In the background the midget, whom I imagined leaping up and down in a padded chair, chanted: "Hola! Hola, Hola!"

"Hello?"

I smiled at the sound of Patrick's voice

"Hi, I got your call."

"Where have you been?" He sounded a little miffed.

"Just around."

"How come you didn't call me?"

"Call you!"

"You know, the phone, those little numbers."

"I didn't want to bother you."

"For a bright kid, you're pretty slow about this. Here's how it works. I call you a couple of times and try to act charming. Then if you're interested in me, you call me back once in a while, you know, to keep my hopes up and everything."

"You wanted me to call you?"

"No. I like sitting around by my phone waiting to hear from you while I rebuild the transmission in my bug and practice swearing in Italian."

"The transmission went out?"

"Yup, but I got her fixed. Went down to the junkyard and bought another one. They leave them lying out in rows so you can look at the outside. Doesn't tell you a thing about the inside. That's a crap shoot. But the year was similar."

"Similar?"

"Yes, similar."

"Does that matter?"

"Most of the pieces seemed to fit in there pretty well. Not too many left over. I'd say it'll be okay. It's within five years."

"Great."

"Anyway, want to have dinner with me?"

"Okay."

"I'll come get you at six and we'll cook here."

"Thanks."

I wondered if I'd get to meet the midget.

33

The midget turned out to be a nine-inch green Amazon parrot, with a vocabulary capable of shocking anyone conversant in romance languages.

"I'm working on his Russian."

"How's he doing?"

"The accent is harder."

Patrick's household's kitchen was considerably neater than mine. He was cooking a large pot of chili, while the parrot sat lovingly on his shoulder, preening the hair behind his left ear. The bird's brown and yellow eyes contracted to pinpoints whenever Patrick walked near to me. The parrot flattened himself against Patrick's chin and made threatening gestures, his neck outstretched in my direction.

"He's jealous. If you came too close he'd bite."

"Is he an attack parrot?"

"Oh, he wouldn't bite you, he'd bite me!"

"Why?"

"He considers me his mate."

"Really?"

"He's a little confused."

"I guess."

"In the wild he'd try to scare his buddy away from danger by nipping. Of course that hurts a lot less when the love object has feathers!"

"I'll keep my distance."

"I'll put him up when I get done here."

"Want some help?"

"I want you to pour yourself a large glass of wine and tell me how your research is going."

"Okay. Then will you swear at me in Italian for a while?"

"What?"

"That's what you said you've been working on, other than the transmission."

"Too true."

Patrick and I ate dinner on the sofa, balancing plates on arms and laps. The multilingual parrot hung upside down happily from the top of his cage exclaiming, "Bad bird! Hola! Bad bird! Ouch! Ouch! Bad bird!"

"He does know some English," Patrick explained needlessly.

"Who was it that answered the phone this afternoon?"

"One of my housemates, Sandy. He's a History major. He teaches rock climbing, instructs at the National Outdoor Leadership School, comes home with frostbitten toes every Christmas—that kind of thing."

"Dark-haired, good looking?"

"Black tips on his toes? Want to meet him?"

"No. I already know him."

"Really?"

"Yup, he ignores me while I swoon. Who else do you live with?"

"Elliot, who claims he's studying Business but spends most of his time smoking dope and watching old movies."

"Elliot Parks?"

"Yup. We call him 'Stoneman.'"

"I've had a class with him. He looks so straight."

"One of the more twisted individuals I've met. He can both drink and smoke me under the table, which is not a pleasant experience."

"You smoke too?"

"Only dope. And only on Fridays of months containing an R."

"Really?"

"Just how naive are you?"

I didn't answer.

"We're going to have to work on your corruption."

"Can I use being underage as an excuse?"

"Works for me. But, what are you underage for, exactly?"

Patrick neatly dodged the pillow I threw at him, but tipped over his drink and we spent the next few minutes clearing up the dishes while the parrot imitated a lovesick rooster.

We sat down and he said, "I was kind of hoping you'd make an effort at seducing me."

"I don't know how." I could feel the hair start to rise on my neck.

"Have you ever had sex?"

"No."

"Ever gone necking?"

"No."

"We'll have to start at the beginning."

"Where's that?"

"No wonder Sandy ignores you! We sit on the sofa, watch TV and hold hands."

Which is what we did, until halfway through the movie I fell asleep, his arm resting over my shoulder. About two in the morning I woke up and found myself still on the sofa with a blanket, but Patrick was nowhere in sight. I both missed him and was relieved. Thinking of the raised eyebrows I would provoke on returning home, I took the blanket and made myself a bed behind one of the armchairs. Sometime after dawn I awoke to voices in the living room.

"Sweetheart... Honey! Stop that!"

"What?"

"Hola! HOLA!"

"Very funny."

"Good morning. Sleep well?" It was Patrick and the bird.

"I want a shower."

"No. I like dirty girls."

"It's too early, Patrick. Cough up a towel."

"Okay."

We went out to breakfast. Patrick's favorite breakfast joint was just past the bridge and over the railroad tracks. He ordered a chili cheese omelet for both of us, saying, "You'll love this."

"That's what they all say."

We were walking to the bug when he stated, "So, you've slept with your first man. What did you think?"

"Remarkably dull."

"I'm crushed."

"Sorry. The shower was great though."

"I shouldn't let you get away with this. You're pretty cocky for a virgin."

I punched him on the shoulder, and he threw an arm around my neck and grabbed the offending hand.

"Half nelson. Did I tell you I was the Ketchum wrestling champ both junior and senior year in high school?"

"No." I said with some effort, "You skipped that part in your autobiography."

He released me and we got in the car.

"Patrick, have you gone out with a lot of girls?"

"Not too many. I am, technically, a virgin as well," he said, rather grandly, "but I've checked all the other stuff off my list!"

"What?"

"I'm only human." He made a lecherous, leering caricature, one shoulder pushed up sharply.

"Not that, idiot!"

"Well, like they say in any crime, it comes down to motive and opportunity."

"Be serious."

"I am being serious. You want the short answer?"

"Give me the long one."

"I wasn't really old enough for a relationship in high school. I was shy. The women in France wanted rich guys, which I was not. When I was welding there were no women I could recognize as such on the oil rigs. And I haven't found anyone I really liked that much here at school. I've gone out some, but most women seem more worried about their hair than they are about talking with you. I like smart people. I know for a fact that women are just as clever as men, and I do not understand why they like to hide it so well. Most of the women here have never had a job, don't know anything about life and are spoiled to death."

"Do you like me? I've never had a job."

"No, I just like to drive endlessly and you keep me company."

"Wretch."

"Of course I like you. I'm crazy about you."

"How come?"

"Beats me."

"Cad."

34

Patrick and I made plans to have dinner together again before he dropped me off at home. To my relief, neither Sandra nor Roger was home. I neglected to look for messages.

Sandra and Roger arrived very shortly before I left for the evening.

"Where were you last night?" Sandra asked.

"I stayed over at Patrick's house. We fell asleep watching TV."

"Really?"

"Yes. How are you and Roger doing?"

"Fine. But look, I'm not happy about this. You haven't been really at home for weeks, and we need to clean up the house. It's not Roger's and my job to take messages for you and be housemaids. If we're going to live together you have to do your part."

"I'm sorry. There's just been a lot going on and I haven't even had time to cook anything, never mind clean up."

"Do you think it's right for us to have to do everything?"

"Not at all. It's just that. . ."

"Did you look at the messages?"

"No, I was studying. I forgot."

"Your mother called again and said you were supposed to call her. Did you do it?"

"No."

"Come on! You can't just ignore her like that. I know you've been seeing a lot of this guy, but she's your mother."

"I don't think you understand."

"I might not, but I'm sick of answering the phone."

"I guess you're right."

"Roger and I have been talking about it and we think it might be best if we got a place for ourselves."

"But we have a lease until June."

"*You* have a lease until June."

"But this place is too big for me alone."

"You could find other roommates."

"I don't want to. How about if we get the landlord to sign the lease over to you two and I'll find a different place?"

"We can think about it."

"All right."

"Don't forget to call your mother."

I didn't answer her.

Patrick picked me up as promised, but I was feeling flat. Depressed and tired. He tried to make conversation, and then gave up and let the silence lie still. Finally he asked, "Are you mad at me?"

"No, I'm just worried."

"What about?"

"I'm in trouble. My mom is mad, my roommates are mad, and even my brother is a little mad."

"What did you do?"

"I'm not sure."

"Give me an example."

"I can't. Let's just drop it."

"Okay."

Patrick's roommates were home that night, Sandy limping moodily around the kitchen and Elliot watching a game show on T.V. with headphones. I was feeling shy. Even the bird was quiet. After dinner I asked Patrick to take me home. He dutifully drove me and when we arrived, he got out and stood with me on the sidewalk, giving me a quick hug and saying, "Don't take it so hard. It will all work out."

"Right."

I spent a lot of hours in the library that month, researching the Samosa dictatorship in Nicaragua through the government documents. The diplomatic reports read like a novel. It was intensely interesting. I wrote the three drafts of my paper with vigor, telling Patrick about the evils of Central American politics as we studied together.

I thought a lot about my father, about primary sources that would tell me more. I wanted to go to the library in Ketchum and find more about the 10th Mountain. The school library had no information that the *Blizzard* magazines hadn't told me already.

I spoke with Judy Crawford back in Idaho, and Paula as well. The house was fine. I had bills forwarded to Colorado Springs and solemnly paid them out of Lew's account, guarding it jealously. Still it bothered me, as the efforts of his thrift were being eroded. I decided to get a job.

Patrick was not enthusiastic about this project. He said, "Your grades will suffer."

I ignored him. The weekend I turned twenty-one I got a job as a cocktail waitress at a restaurant with a bar. It was downtown, about twelve blocks from school. I told Patrick about it proudly.

"I'm dying to see you in one of those short little black dresses with the white apron. I'll be your best customer."

"Stop it. It's a jeans and shirt sort of place."

"You'll get better tips if you leave off the shirt."

"How would you know?"

"Just guessing."

"Right."

"We should drive back on the break between classes and get your dad's Subaru. It would be safer for you at night. In the meantime, I'll pick you up after work."

"You don't have to do that."

"Give it a rest."

35

Classes got out on Wednesday at noon. I handed in my last paper, Patrick took his final exam on eighteenth century Italian literature, and we were in the bug and rolling at one. At eleven that night we stopped, just east of Salt Lake City and got a motel room.

"I thought you didn't do this kind of thing—you know, motel rooms."

"We can check in under one name. You pick it. That's the way it happens in the movies. Either that, or you can wait out here blushing in central Utah while I get the key." He leered at me.

"Stop it."

He went in by himself, leaving me blushing, as predicted, in the bug. He returned triumphantly.

"I told them that I was a Mormon and my other wives would be arriving soon."

"Great."

"It's the perfect cover—they'll never suspect a thing."

He found the door and opened it.

"Patrick, it only has one bed."

"Sweetheart, do you think I'm stupid?"

"But what about all the other wives?"

"Very funny. You want the shower first?"

"Okay."

I padded around the room restlessly in my flannel nightgown while Patrick showered. I was nervous, no surprise, not entirely sure what I had gotten myself into.

He emerged, still toweling off his hair, but decently clothed and sat down on the bed. He patted the other side of it and said, "Come here, I'm not going to bite you."

"I know, but I'm nervous."

"Me too."

"Do you think we ought to? You know. . .?"

"You mean act like married people?"

I nodded.

"Well if you want to, we can. Just one problem though."

"What?"

"Can't find the remote."

I tackled him and started to punch him.

"Careful now, no violence. You'll have to be gentle with me."

I lay down beside him and he kissed me, saying, "Besides, if you want to have sex we'd have to go out. I'm ill-equipped."

"That doesn't sound good."

Now he was blushing. "I didn't mean that!"

"Oh."

"I just didn't want you to think I was one of those fast guys. It seemed presumptuous, you know, making assumptions, that kind of thing."

"I'll translate. You were too embarrassed to buy condoms?"

"Right."

"Good thing. You were scaring me to death anyway."

"I have a better idea. We'll go to phase two."

"What's that?"

"I'll show you."

"Oh."

At two in the morning I woke up suddenly, as if a shot had gone off. I listened carefully to the sounds outside. There was nothing. I got up and investigated the bathroom. Patrick moved in his sleep and I froze to the wall. I took the leftover towels and my coat and made a bed behind the door.

I woke up in the morning. Patrick was standing over me, looking at my makeshift bed. "Was it that bad?"

"It's not that. But I woke up and I was afraid." I wasn't quite sure how to describe the early morning scare.

He looked at me thoughtfully. Then he said, "Well, rise and shine. We should hit the road."

"Okay."

The route from Salt Lake took us through Twin Falls, across the Snake River once more. From there the drive to Lew's house seemed to take no time. I brought Lew's cannister of ashes along for the trip. It seemed right for all of us to visit his home together. Patrick and I drove through Hailey in light snow, passing the chapel. I thought about my puppy. He would be walking now. I'd have to call see if Sadie was accepting visitors.

We unlocked Lew's house and turned off the security system. All was in order. Paula had watered the geraniums. I put Lew's cannister up on the shelf again, next to the wooden skis. Patrick sat down in Lew's chair and said, "It's nice to be back."

"I'll say."

Patrick puttered around in Lew's knife collection for a while, looking at the sharpening stones. I decided my project for the afternoon would be washing the windows, which were still streaked and grimy from Lew's smoking. I found a bucket, three sponges and two rubber squeegee tools with handles.

"Do you want some help?" Patrick asked.

"No thanks. Were you going to visit your folks?"

"They don't know I'm here, but I should probably go over."

"Why don't you do that."

"And leave you by yourself?"

"Please, Patrick, I'm fine by myself and I want to get this done."

"Okay, but if I were you, I'd do the standard male thing about housework."

"Sleep?"

"No, put it off."

"This is a very male house! See you whenever."

"Okay, I'll give you a call later."

He left and I continued washing windows.

After a while I got tired and went upstairs. I lay down on Lew's bed and looked out the window into the snow, thinking about the first time I had seen the bed and all the reading material he had lying around. I'd thought it was dirty at the time. I remembered the photos, incredibly round women, taut, full, tanned and white. I wondered why Patrick even hung around with me if there were women who looked like that. After looking down at my dirty clothes and grimy wrists, I began unbuttoning my shirt. As I walked along Lew's loft I leisurely stripped it off. By the end of my stroll I stood over the upstairs washer, remembering my dad. What an odd thought. I stuffed the clothes in, planning to wash them after I got done with my shower. I turned the sauna on.

Naked and clean, I lay on my back in the sauna, thinking of Patrick. He was a lot of fun. I'd never thought being with a man would be fun. I thought you had to be on guard every moment. Men, in both my imagination and my experience, were dangerous, scary, and violent. Patrick was none of these. I wondered if he was going to get tired of being nice, or if he was just that way. I wondered about my mother. I remembered her kicking me and calling me a slut. I could just imagine what she would say right now. Not a pretty thought. I changed the subject for myself.

After a while I got out of the sauna. I turned the washing machine on and rinsed myself with cold water. Then, once more, I walked through my father's upper floor and lay in his bed under the down comforter. I looked out the window, heard the furnace start and thought of Lew. Chances were, he would approve of my lounging.

Patrick was standing over the bed when I woke. He looked down at me and said unnecessarily, "I came back."

I pulled the comforter up to my neck and said sleepily, "Hi."

"Don't do that."

I put the comforter down.

"You are so lovely, I can barely stand it."

"Patrick, don't say things like that."

"It's true. Come look for yourself—I'll bet you've never done that."

I was still feeling shy, but I dragged the comforter along and followed him. He was standing in the bathroom in front of the mirror. He had taken his shirt off and the outline of his chest appeared wide in the deepening light. I held the comforter in front of me.

"Come here. Look in the mirror."

"I can't. I'll be too ashamed."

"Why? You're lovely."

"I don't think so."

"Why ever not? Your back is like a sculpture." He was facing the mirror holding me now, arms around my waist. The comforter had fallen to the floor. He turned sideways and took me with him. Regretfully, I looked. The mirror held the image of us together: he deeply tanned, my unexplored breasts white against his chest. He gently pushed me away to look, but I dropped my eyes, ashamed.

"I can't."

"That's enough then."

"Okay," I said sadly.

We walked back to Lew's bed.

"Don't feel bad, it's okay."

"You think so?"

"Yup. Come here."

Patrick finished getting undressed and lay down with me. I had never seen a man naked before and I was afraid to look. I lay close to him, feeling both strange and normal. He moved against me and I was afraid for a moment, but he asked, "Are you okay?"

"I think so."

Patrick stroked my hair, arranging the still-wet strands behind my ear. He took my face in both hands and kissed me, opening his mouth. I could feel his breath on my cheek, moving my drying hair.

"I lived through my purchase at the drug store, but I don't know how to do this either, so let's take it from the top, okay?"

I laughed at him and asked, "Want to give me the ten cent tour?"

He sighed, moving closer and said, "Shut up."

"Okay."

"Can I touch you?"

"Aren't you?"

He smiled and kissed me again, mouth open, his breath quickening.

After a while he asked, "You ready for me?"

"How would I know?"

"You want me?"

"Yes, please."

"That's my girl. You tell me if it hurts, okay?"

The burning was intense for a moment and I almost called for him to stop. But instead I put my head to his chest so he could not see and held him there, because I wanted him so badly.

36

I was asleep when Patrick rolled over and hugged me. I wasn't sure for a moment where I was. He casually moved his arm by my head and my vision blurred. I startled and sat up, looking at him. The nighttime ran faster for a moment and then slowed eerily. I saw a flash beside my head and the image of a hand descending flickered by. Then a series of them darted like swallows. I cringed.

"What?" Patrick was awake.

"I don't know."

"Come here," he said sleepily.

"I can't."

"What?"

He started to move toward me, but I was still disoriented by my visions, not sure what was real.

"Please, stay still. Don't come any closer."

I got out of the bed, looking for my clothes, still wet in the washer. I could not think. There were others downstairs, but too far away. Like weapons unloaded, no use. I wanted to run. I needed to be by myself. I felt it was not safe here.

Patrick moved in the bed and reached for me, not understanding. I shied away, moving backward to keep him in view. He was awake now, upset at my fear, trying to help. He followed me as I sank to the floor, gagging, feeling like I was strangling.

"What's the matter?" Patrick asked, kneeling by me.

I felt as if the air in the room had compressed. I gagged again.

"Please, just. Please stay. It's not you. But you have to stay please away."

"Okay. What's the matter?"

"I don't know."

"You want me to go?"

"No! Please don't go. I love you, I want you to stay. Just don't come any closer and I'll be fine.

He was fully awake and looked thoroughly worried. He handed me a collection of bedclothes, moving very slowly. Then he sat on the bed, looking at me in the dark.

I said, "I'm sorry." Then I dragged the covers to the corner and curled up on the floor shivering, finally rocking myself to sleep.

I awoke on the floor close to morning with a hung-over feeling. I got up and washed my face. It was cold in the bathroom. I felt sore and tired from the night. I went back into Lew's room. Patrick stirred and woke, asking, "What's up?"

"Not too much."

"How are you doing?"

"I'm okay. How are you?"

"Fine, thanks."

He looked me in the face and said, "You know this is ridiculous, right?"

"What?"

"We lose our mutual virginity, you wake up in the middle of the night seeing ghosts, sleep on the floor and then appear mostly naked in front of me, your legs still covered in blood. The ridiculous part is none of that, but the fact that we're talking like we're standing in an elevator."

"You've got a point. Any suggestions?"

"You come here and get warmed up and then we take a shower together and go out to breakfast."

"Deal."

We drove Lew's Subaru that morning, me at the wheel, Patrick reaching for his seat belt.

"It's the law," he said.

"Right," I answered, putting it in four-wheel drive.

Outside the door of the diner Patrick finally asked: "You joining a convent?"

"What?"

"Didn't appear that your first foray into sin was too delicious."

"Stop!"

"Come on, the fragile male ego is taking another beating here."

"Patrick. I am delighted. Honestly, I lived through it! I never expected to enjoy it. For heaven's sake, what do you want?"

"Practice?"

"Brother."

"Ouch," said Patrick.

The waitress smiled at him and seated us.

"You know, I never asked you where you were last night."

"Other things on your mind?"

I ignored him and asked, "Where are your parents?"

"Cross-country skiing in Stanley."

"So what did you do last night before you came home? You were out a while."

"Well, of course I had to go shopping, that took some time. That kind of purchase isn't so easy in a town where you know everybody. You know, you have to wait for a salesgirl you didn't sit behind in third grade, that kind of thing."

"What else?"

"You're pretty nosy!"

"Sorry."

"I was only teasing. I went and talked with the guys at the shop. We're going to be building some major projects this year. I wanted to ask them how the schedule is looking."

"Are you going to work for your dad after you graduate?"

"I don't know. He'd probably give me a job, but that's not a good idea for too long. I'd rather find something more in my field."

"What exactly do you do in 'your field'?"

"Not really sure, but it would have to be with a pretty good-sized company, probably a contractor working internationally. That's the only way you need multilingual people. I've got experience with construction, but that's usually local in scale. I think it's going to take some hunting around to find a job I like. But first, something to pay the bills. Then I'll wait for the one I want for keeps. I've already sent out résumés to several big firms."

"Where?" I asked, worried.

"Big cities mostly. I'll just have to wait and see who writes back. What are you going to do with your degree? You'll have to be answering these questions yourself next year."

"This is really embarrassing, but you're the first person I've known that has actually had a job."

"I don't have one now."

"You know what I mean. My family all worked, but none of them had jobs. I think they were what you call 'independently wealthy'.

"Finally! I've found a rich woman!"

"Sorry, my mother's generation has all the income for eons and in my generation it gets split about a zillion ways. None of them have earned a cent that I can tell, so it will be slim pickings by the time it trickles down to me. I might be able to take you out for a soda when I'm forty, if I play my cards right."

"Only if you are very very good. . ."

"In any case, you're right, I should be thinking about it. I did volunteer work this fall at Legal Services just to get a feel for it, but I think law and social work are both out."

"How come?"

"This is embarrassing."

"Even better."

"I'm not sure I have enough sympathy for the very poor and I'm not sure I have enough admiration for the guys trying to get richer than Croesus."

"Who?"

"A really rich guy."

"Okay. So what does that leave?"

"I could teach riding."

"Bad idea. If it's anything like teaching skiing, people want you to do it for nothing until you've spent so much money getting good, never mind famous, that you can never recoup your investment. Then, even if you make a living it's teaching rich people with no talent, entertaining them until they get bored or un-rich, whichever comes first."

"That's pretty pessimistic."

"But true. I grew up in a ski town, remember?"

"Well, there's always waitressing!"

"I keep telling you, and I now consider myself an authority, take your shirt off—you'll do better."

"I'm not doing so bad. I got fifteen in tips the other night."

"And two-fifty an hour wages?"

"About that."

"So, five bucks an hour?"

"Kind of."

"Do you know how much Lew made per hour working for my Dad?"

"No."

"Twenty an hour."

"And my family thought he was poor."

"He wasn't wealthy for around here."

"How much is that a year?"

"Thirty-six thousand, give or take."

I thought about this. My mother got more from her trust fund than Lew made at his best job. Her life was salaried indefinitely for simply existing, not for working. And my grandfather had always paid for extras. I hesitated to say this to Patrick.

"So if I kept waitressing at five dollars an hour I'd make nine thousand a year. That's about two hundred and fifty more a month than I live on now."

"But you don't pay health insurance or keep a car."

"Right. How do people do it?"

"It's not easy."

"I'm going to have to work on my sympathy for the poor."

"Your choice."

We went home to Lew's place and fiddled around in the house. We spent the afternoon working on arranging the tools in the garage.

Toward evening I was restless again, thinking of last night. I wanted Patrick to be happy with me. I was ashamed of my midnight terrors, and both anticipated and dreaded the coming night.

Sitting on the sofa, Patrick leaned down and kissed me for a leisurely moment. As I was wondering how soon he would get around to the sex part, he took a deep breath through his nose and blew out sharply. The air came out my nose.

"Pay attention!" he said.

"How romantic. Where'd you learn that?"

"Third grade."

"The salesgirl at the drugstore?"

"Exactly."

"Was she cute?"

"Very."

"Rat."

"Sweetheart, I'm not an expert, but it seems like you're worrying too much. I think you should relax and see what happens."

He pulled me a little closer on the sofa and held me quietly until I said, "I'm worried if I don't make you happy something bad will happen."

"What bad?"

"I'm not sure. I just feel like I need to keep an eye on things."

"Is that why you get scared when you wake up?"

"How'd you know?"

"It's not exactly subtle. Does it always happen?"

"It's different when I'm alone; then I just can't feel *anything* if I get upset. But other than that, I only feel safe when I'm by myself."

"What's it like when you're with someone?"

"That's when it gets scary. I get nervous if I'm not sure I'm doing the right thing."

"What's the right thing?"

"Whatever they want. But sometimes I just can't make myself do what they want. It's too scary. I see things that aren't there."

He raised his eyebrows.

"You think I'm crazy?"

"I don't think it's that simple, but I'm worried about you and I've got an idea."

"What?"

"We've both lived this long without sex, right?"

"Right."

"A couple more months won't hurt."

"Are you mad at me?"

"No, but I think it would be better."

"You don't like me?"

"No, I love you."

"Oh."

A few minutes later, while I sat miserably on the bed awaiting his departure, Patrick emerged from the bathroom in his shorts. He said, "Let's go to bed."

I was leaking again and irritated by it. I wiped my eyes and said miserably, "I thought you weren't going to sleep with me."

"I didn't say that, I just said I wanted to wait till you get over being scared of me, or whatever it is you're scared of, before we make love again. For a smart girl you're pretty slow tonight."

"I'll work on it."

He sat down and patted my shoulder, looking at my blotched face. "God, you're soggy, drenched."

"Is kissing out too?"

"I'll make an exception in this case, but only if you ask nicely."

"I hate you."

"Too bad. This is supposed to be fun. That's what they claim anyway. I want you to go see a therapist when we get back to school; just on account of your dad dying you probably ought to get some counseling. It can be helpful."

"Great."

After a while we slept.

37

In Colorado Springs a few weeks later I walked home from school at dusk. Lew's car was sitting outside my house. I was off that night, but Patrick and I had settled on spending weekends together and talking on the phone in the evenings. It was the only way to get any work done.

I hadn't told my mother about him, or talked with her about a therapist. In fact I had still been avoiding talking with her at all. I just didn't know what to say. Anything I really thought looked like dangerous territory.

I had gone to the school counseling center, guiltily sitting in the lobby with victims of flu and hangover, waiting for my appointment. I was sure everybody was looking at me.

The therapist was a woman with long blonde hair. She shook my hand and then sat behind the desk again. She took notes on a printed sheet while we talked.

"What can I help you with?"

"It's kind of complicated."

"Try to explain."

"I think it has something to do with sex."

"Oh?"

"It's okay if I'm alone, but if I'm with someone I get really nervous when I wake up, and I think I see things."

"Bad dreams?"

"No, not really dreams, things that aren't there." I was having trouble explaining the problem. She was writing faster. It was making me nervous.

"What else?"

"Well, my father died in December."

"Were you close?"

"Not exactly."

"Your relationship with your mother?"

"She supports me, but. . ." I don't think she heard me.

"That's good." She seemed pleased. "How are you doing in school?"

"Fine."

I was glad Patrick thought this was useful, but I was having trouble getting the hang of it. I tried to be direct.

"Sex is a problem."

"You have had coitus?"

"Excuse me?

"Intercourse. You have had intercourse?"

"Yes." *But not recently*, I thought.

"What seems to be the problem?"

"Um, I, well, I'm not sure what the problem is, but my boyfriend says he doesn't want to have sex anymore before we get it figured out."

"Is your boyfriend abusive?"

"Pardon me?"

"Your boyfriend, does he boss you around or hit you, isolate you or refuse you transportation?"

"Well, I actually hit him more than he hits me and I'd say we boss each other around about equally. He drives more than I do, but I have my dad's car here now so I can get around if he's busy."

She put a little check on her form, looking gratified.

At the end of the session she said, "The college does not offer long-term counseling, but I can schedule you for three appointments if you think that would be useful."

"Okay."

The receptionist made the appointments, one each for the first Tuesday of the month: April, May and June. My first session had not been the cathartic miracle I'd expected. Considering that it had taken me a month to gain the courage to go, I was disappointed.

38

When I got home there was a letter in my mother's handwriting, waiting on the hall table. Usually around the first week or two of the month she sent a check with my living allowance. This envelope, however, had an ominous weight, as if several pages were enclosing the check.

But I was wrong. When I opened the envelope, I found it contained not a check, but a closely typewritten letter reiterating the list of my personal faults. She was thorough, leaving nothing out in the litany of my numerous shortcomings.

It was clear my mother was tired of getting no entertainment for her investment. She was looking for greener pastures. The closing paragraphs of the hefty missive read, "I only detail the above as symptoms of your apparent lack of concern over the use of other people's money, time and effort. You did not see fit to visit me over the holidays, instead insisting on traveling to Idaho on the spur of the moment, utterly at the beck and call of a man whom you knew to be abusive and unstable in character.

"Now we hear that he has left his 'estate' to you, whatever that might amount to, and I cannot but assume you have made the choice as to which side of the family you wish to be associated with. I have done my share in supporting you over the years and I deserve more credit than you are apparently willing to allow."

She continued, "I am sick to death of your neglecting my phone calls. Your assertion of being busy, while I support you in the lap of luxury, is absurd. I hope you will have leisure to contemplate what you have given up by your actions. I must focus on more productive areas of my life.

"As you have reached your majority, I am not obligated to pay your tuition, rent, food or other bills. I decline these as of now, and neither do I wish contact with you in the future. I will make a clean start, remaining sadder, but far wiser. . . "

Clearly, my mother was taking no prisoners in this battle. For a few moments I was stunned. But I had perhaps expected it all along. If nothing else, my mother demanded absolute loyalty. The previous list of winnowed chaff—husband, brother, pets—was now lengthened by the addition of her child.

Still, it was not fun standing in the exhaust of her departure. My skin felt flushed, like it was swelling. I sat down in the hallway, a disquieting crack opening in my defenses. It was quite possible that she was right. I was, like my uncle and father, very bad.

I went upstairs and looked at the razor. It was not sharp enough.

I should have stayed where I was, or called Patrick. It was the wrong thing to do, going for a walk. Something to be added to my list of failures. My mother would not be happy. But then again she would never know.

I wished I had brought Lew's ashes home with me.

I went out the door without my coat and started to walk. Traffic hummed, but I didn't notice it. Someone honked at me when I crossed the street, but I didn't think why. I must have been out almost an hour when I started to feel the chill of the night. I was beginning to wake up, realizing vaguely where I was: about fifteen blocks west of school. I knew the street name, but I didn't know the houses. A car passed me, slowing. It rolled to a stop ahead. One brake light was missing, but the other brightened the curb.

The man in the passenger's seat put down the window and stuck his head out. His hair was very short. He looked at me hard. Then he smiled, teeth yellow in the glare. I stopped and made an abrupt turn back the way I had come. The smiling man said something to the driver, who reversed the car. I cut across the yard to my left and reluctantly began to pick up the pace.

Part of me just wanted to stop. The image of halting and letting the car catch up was tempting. I imagined myself simply standing passively, letting them approach. The future would be out of my hands.

Then my imagination took another speedy preview and I started to run.

As I took the first few steps I heard a single car door slam, but not the second. The back yard of the house was not fenced. I found the alley and sprinted down it, not taking time to think, hearing the scuffle of running steps behind. The alley was lined with chain link. Headlights appeared in front of me and I ran faster, thinking of the safety of a single witness.

I was on top of the car before I recognized it. The second man opened the door and got out. When he started walking toward me I backed up. Knowing I should start making some noise, I opened my mouth, but I could not bring myself to scream.

The man with yellow teeth closed the rear exit, breathing hard from his run, exuding a smell of cigarettes. The second circled alongside the car. He was not tall, had longer, dark hair. He held his hands up, palms toward me and said, "You stay still now, we're not going to hurt you."

"The bitch can run." The out-of-breath man sounded angry. "An athlete."

I didn't answer.

"Get in the car."

In that fractured moment I would have obeyed, but I could not. The men were receding in my vision. My feet stayed rooted firmly to the ground. I couldn't move. There was a familiar flickering around the edges of my eyesight, and when the men moved I wasn't sure if it was real, or a vision. When the taller man hit me I guessed it was real as I felt the skin of my cheek split and my back hit the chain link. But it didn't hurt.

The man held his knuckles as though they hurt. "Get in the car."

I was fully alert now, getting my feet under me. As my vision cleared the night appeared crystalline. I could see every detail. When either of the men moved it appeared to happen slowly. I bent my knees, watching them carefully. I decided, panic gone, that they would need to kill me before I got in the car.

As the first man took a slow step toward me, something hit the fence, making the mesh sway. I was focused on the man in motion and didn't look back, but the depth of the growl that came from behind me spoke of size.

The first man took a step back and said to his partner, "Goddamn dog!"

Both men took a step back as the dog hit the fence the second time. Then, as if angered by their fear, they moved in again, fast.

Instinctively I turned, hugging the top rail of the fence, which was chest high. The dog's teeth snapped in the air by my ear as I threw a leg over. It was easier than getting on a horse bareback, but the fall on the other side hurt. The shepherd, intent on the rush from the men, ignored me and launched itself once more at the wire.

I lay on the ground for a long moment as the dog continued to snarl and rush the fence over the top of me. One of the men kicked the base where I lay, sending shivers down the metal fabric. This set the dog to barking furiously. After a moment car doors slammed and headlights washed the yard. The noise of the engine receded into the gloom, carrying the predators off into the night.

Of course this left me alone with the dog. He quieted when the two potential intruders left, but seemed at a loss about what to do with the actual intruder. He stared at me from a crouched position, lips slightly raised. As I moved, he growled very softly. I sat still again. After a while, the chill started to deepen, cold trickling down my back from the air and seeping through my thighs from the ground. I sat there for a long time, until the dog lay down, eyes still intent on me.

"Can I go home now?"

At the word "go" he wagged his tail.

Great, I thought, *I'm getting frostbite and he suddenly wants to play.*

As I thought of my striped shepherd, my current shepherd sat up and stared, eyes dark and bright in the moonlight. But he did not object as I got up and walked carefully along the fence to the gate.

About halfway down the block I heard a car. In that moment I would have done anything to go back to the dog's yard, but the car went harmlessly past. In another block I found a convenience store. It was open, but I waited in the shadows, too shy to walk in. I was afraid my cut face and general appearance would cause a stir. There was a phone booth on the edge of the parking lot. I searched my pockets for change and deposited the coins. Finally the phone was answered.

"I need a taxi."

"Where are you?"

I told him.

Patrick found me, but had to open the door of the phone booth to do so. I sat huddled motionless on the floor. He took one look at me and said, "We are going to the hospital."

I am sure they were very nice at the hospital. But it's a miracle that if they had a psychiatric ward, they didn't lock me in it. I was acting crazy. My injuries were minor; that was quickly established. The hypothermia was more serious than the cut. But I was afraid of the doctor.

I begged Patrick not to leave me as the doctor entered the examination room. I hid my face in his shirt as the man probed my cheek. Visions polluted my judgment. I was not sure what was real. At one moment I saw hands raised to strike, at another I could not breathe. It was intolerable. When the doctor persisted and Patrick would not protect me, I moved across the room, eyes quickly circling between the two men, watching each of their movements carefully.

Patrick was stoic, talking to the doctor calmly. I was not included in the conversation, but I was thoroughly occupied with keeping track of them.

"Has she taken any illegal drugs?" asked the doctor.

"Not likely at all."

"She's not acting right. It could be the result of a concussion, but the pupils' response to light is normal, so I doubt it."

I thought about him touching my face and took a step back.

The doctor tried to get my attention.

"Did the men do anything else to you besides hit you?"

"No. I want to go home. I need to leave." I edged nearer the wall of the small examination room, eyeing the door.

Patrick nodded. "We'll go home in a while."

I was furious.

The doctor ignored me and talked to Patrick. "I can't find much clinically wrong with her, but she's paranoid, close to hysterics, and I'm not comfortable sedating her because of the possibility of concussion. She won't let me do any more detailed examination."

Damn right, I thought.

"I'm going to give you the number of our social worker. It would be a good idea to do follow up on this. There's a support group for victims of attack, mostly women. It would be a good idea for her to attend a few sessions."

The doctor gave Patrick the number of the social worker and then, to my great relief, allowed us to leave. I watched the details of our exit carefully, cataloguing the occupants of the emergency room.

Back in the car I said, "You think I'm crazy."

"No."

He was silent for a while and I asked, "What are you thinking?"

"Actually, it might just be your eyes, but sometimes it's amazing how much you look like your dad."

"Was he crazy too?"

"At times, yes. But he'd get violent when he was over the edge, not just scared. And he had the training to do it. He wasn't really there at times; he looked a long way away and it would be as if he'd see things that weren't there either. Or, he'd get spooked if you startled him. And then he'd be mad.

"There was part of that anger he just couldn't stay away from. He knew it would come out if he drank, but it was like he wanted it to. It was really weird, because it didn't look like any fun at all for him. I can't explain it. He just couldn't stay away from it."

I couldn't answer that, but after a while I said, "Sorry."

"That's not the point. Everybody knew he had been through a lot. You don't live through what he did and come out looking like Mr. Suburban. But it would have been easier on everybody if he had gotten help. Would have saved a lot of black eyes. But we still liked him, and his troubles were a lot more trouble to him than to any of us. He didn't have to be perfect. Neither do you, but you can't live the rest of your life like this. It's going to be too much of a problem."

"You sure?" I did not believe him.

"You're impossible! Come here! We need to get some ice on your face. You look like you've been in a barroom fight."

"Chip off the old block."

"I guess."

"You going to the support group?"

"I'm leaving. I'm going to my dad's house."

"*Now* you're acting crazy."

"I'm not talking about leaving tonight. I just don't want to be here anymore. My mom's dumped me, my roommates want to live by themselves. There are only two more blocks of classes after the break. I'll ask T.K. for an independent study."

"I can't understand you! You'll be all by yourself."

"I want to go home."

"Okay."

39

I left early for the drive back to Idaho, did the trip straight through and arrived at twilight. The thaw was beginning. The streets of Hailey ran with water. Small signs of spring crept along south faces in the valley; the aspen and willows showed traces of color.

At Lew's place, tiny leaves appeared at the base of the south-facing stucco: future clumps of hollyhocks. He had been a gardener. The melting of the snow also uncovered a whole new generation of my father's legacy. The yard was another vast collection area for gleaned items. Paula came over and looked at them fondly. She gave me a hug, saying simply, "Providence," and left.

I went in and said "hi" to Lew, patting his box next to the skis. It would not be long before I'd have to give that up as well. I sat on one of the abandoned cars in the back yard, miserably watching the red and gold sunset. No help arrived, no comfort was expected, the phone did not ring. Unaided, I recovered, but I was tired.

A huge lethargy hampered my efforts at clearing Lew's lot. Day by day I forced myself to move things. The Dumpster was ill-fed.

Finally Paula came over. She admired my healing black eye and then said sensibly, "What's the rush? We've all lived with Lew's landscaping for years." She offered to make packets of hollyhock seeds to give to his friends at the memorial. I thanked her and called for the Dumpster to be removed.

I figured out Lew's satellite dish and watched old movies. Patrick called now and then, but other than that the phone was silent. I was angry at my need, waiting for it to ring. After a while I took revenge and quit answering it.

Patrick's mother dropped by one afternoon. I saw the car in

the drive from an upstairs window. I lay on the bed while she knocked on the locked door. After a while she went away.

A day later I looked out and saw another vehicle in the drive: Chuck's white truck. I heard a dog bark and decided to go downstairs. Chuck was at the blue door, hand raised to knock. I opened it. He smiled, refraining from glancing at my face, and said, "I've got something to show you."

He took the lead to his truck, lifted the topper and lowered the tailgate. Sadie's big ears pricked at me and she wagged her tail. She was standing by a plastic dog crate. Within its confines was a tremendous ruckus. The crate had slid sideways on the trip. Chuck put his fingers in the grill to pull it straight. He removed them promptly, exclaiming, "Ouch!"

I said, "You've got someone waiting for me?"

"Yes."

He opened the press release latches on the kennel and I looked inside. Toward the back, ears flattened and eyes peering suspiciously, was my puppy.

"He's a handful," said Chuck.

"Come here," I said.

The pup cowered to the back, looking ready to bite. I retreated a step, averting my eyes, and he looked calmer.

"Can I borrow the crate?"

"Sure. I brought him some food too." He picked up a sack and put it down by the door.

"Thanks." I closed the wire door and picked up the crate, carrying it inside. I heard Chuck's car start and thought, *I haven't even thanked him.* But he was gone before I got back to the door.

I sat down by the air compressor next to the crate and opened it, retreating a few feet. After a while a nose appeared, quickly retracted. The next time the eyes followed, and after that the body came speedily. I knew if he got loose in the house it would be a frightening chase to catch him, so as he darted out I snatched him up and held him. He wiggled desperately, growling in fear, but not attempting to bite me.

"Do you, my friend, have a delicate character as well?"

He lay on my lap, striped rib cage heaving, flattened like a salamander, large eyes looking up. After a few moments he started to move. As I patted him the tip of his brown shepherd-colored tail began to move.

"Good dog."

I named him Luigi after my dad, and tied him by a string to my belt so that every place I went he must go as well. But he was young and needed to sleep so we still watched a lot of movies. He always hated the crate, but became accustomed to being thrust in it for grocery shopping trips. He ate a lot.

I admired my growing companion, sleeping beside Lew's chair. He was double-coated, the longer guard hairs overlapping the downy under. Where the color of the coat changed a curious pinecone effect occurred. He was going to be big. His close-toed feet were massive. I had no doubt that Sadie's passion for the white and presumably handsome Pyrenese rescue dog had been fulfilled.

"Are you a love child, Luigi?"

He wagged his tail and lay on his back, smiling.

"I bet."

I was in the yard when Patrick's mother appeared next. Luigi sat by my leg and growled. She got out of her jeep and walked toward me. I was ashamed of my bad manners the week before, and went to meet her.

"Hi."

"Well there you are! The place is looking good. I can see you've been busy."

"Kind of."

"How are plans for the memorial going?"

"Okay. I'm going to have it here."

"That will be nice. Is your family coming out?"

"I don't know," I lied, pretty sure they weren't.

"Is your phone working?"

"I think so." I lied again: "I've been out a lot."

She lifted her eyebrows. "I talked with Patrick a few days ago."

"How is he?"

"Fine. We had a good chat."

I looked at the ground, hopelessly.

"Patrick asked me to bring you this." She handed me an envelope.

"Thanks."

"You doing okay?"

I looked at my feet again. Luigi wagged his tail. "I think so."

"Okay. Keep in touch."

"Thanks."

Inside the envelope was a neatly cut page from a phone directory: the listings for counselors working in the valley. Three names were circled.

I put the list of therapists by my phone, where it lay with the same effect as a hibernating bear. I ignored it for several days, but it seemed to migrate to the top of the pile. I looked over the circled names of the counselors and their specialties.

Finally, I decided it wouldn't hurt to make a call.

My new therapist's name was Dr. Rice. She worked in a small Victorian house on the main street of Hailey. She didn't have a desk or take notes, but sat plumply in an arm chair with her sandaled feet up on a stool. She rooted out my story with a the dexterity of an anteater.

At the end of the first session I told her I was worried about money.

"Do you have insurance?"

"No."

"Asking your mother for help is not an option?"

"No. I have money from my Dad, but I'm worried about school next year. I want to finish and I'll need it for that."

"That's good thinking. Here's what to do. I want you to apply for a major medical policy; you should have one anyway."

"Okay."

"In the meantime I'd like you to think about joining one of the women's groups I'm running. Group therapy is much less expensive than individual."

The thought of group therapy made me nervous and I didn't say anything.

"But I'd still like to see you twice a week for the first month. You'll just have to cope with the expense. After that your insurance should kick in. Now, what is this about your mother? How come you don't want to ask her for support?"

It appeared that my social life was going to consist of therapy for a while. Leaving the office, I imagined I should be angry at her bossy attitude. But I wasn't.

40

I had to get going on my research for T.K or lose two paid blocks' credit, which I couldn't afford. I'd promised two projects. The first was on the 10th Mountain Division, for personal reasons and because T.K. suggested there was a lot of information on the division in Sun Valley. I was hoping for transcripts of interviews, which T.K. said were especially important. He had reiterated, "Don't accept someone else's opinion of someone else's opinion. Dig out the interviews, look at pictures, digest the tales of several people who were on the scene. Read what they actually had to say. Then come to your own conclusions."

I hadn't settled on the second project. T.K. had been lenient. Leaning back, thinking in his fit-like way for several moments, head cocked, thick tongue repeatedly swabbing his lips, eyes rolling at the ceiling, he had suddenly focused on me and said, "Pick something that intrigues you, then let's see what happens, shall we?"

The library in Ketchum was well-windowed and lined with armchairs, more like a good hotel than a library. I settled into my research, skimming general history books on World War II to get a feel for the subject. I made notes on index cards to keep points separate. It was time-consuming.

Then I started to read about the 10th Mountain Division specifically. I plundered bibliographies for sources. I made lists, many overlapping, then culled them down to one master list. I took it to the librarian and asked for help. She gave it a look.

"We don't have everything on here," she said. "But we do have a good selection of historical photos on the 10th. And lots of interviews. A number of the members of 87th, which was one part of the 10th Mountain, settled here because of the skiing, which was what they knew how to do."

"I've heard that from my father's friends. How many live here in the valley?"

"I think there were forty or so after the war. But not as many now—they're getting on a bit. Some have died and some have moved. The thing that's special about them is that a lot of men from the initial group moved here. The 87th infantry trained together for years before they saw action. They were elite skiers, men recruited specifically for their outdoor ability by the National Ski Patrol. They made up the first part of what later became the 10th Mountain, joining up in Washington State a couple of years before Camp Hale was built in Colorado. The 10th as a whole was a big affair, and it didn't just happen overnight. The 87th were the first guys in. What is your father's name?"

I told her.

"You're Lew Pierce's daughter. He was one of the decorated ones. A bronze star, I think. I read that he died in the winter. I'm sorry."

"Thank you. Did you know him?"

"No, not personally. He wasn't a library sort of guy. But we have several interviews mentioning him. He was one of the 87th that came from out East, wasn't he?"

"He taught skiing at Dartmouth before the war."

"Then he would have come out with Walter Prager. That was top of the line."

"I don't know." The name sounded familiar. "Can I look at the interviews sometime?"

"Certainly. I'll get the ones that are here for you, but the set isn't complete right now. Some of them are on display at the Lodge this month with the collection of historic ski pictures. The collections overlap. You might want to take a trip out there and have a look. But I'll get the ones we have."

She returned with a small stack of documents.

I read the interviews in the library, as they could not be checked out. The men interviewed talked about the Aleutian Islands in 1943. I had no idea where these were and had to look it up. They were off the Alaskan coast.

The interview folder included some pictures of landing craft. Not a bit of snow in sight. I could see I was going to have to improve my general sense of history to put this in perspective. I went back to my books.

The 87th, the books told me, was formed in 1941. Over the next few years this elite corps, which included my father, had been increased to about two thousand. They trained at Mt. Rainier in Washington State, but their first mission in the Aleutian Islands had nothing to do with snow or mountains.

The army, apparently lacking anyone else to do the job, detailed the 87th to the Aleutians to subdue a Japanese force reportedly hiding there. It was a fiasco. The Japanese had secretly departed before the soldiers arrived. Mapping of the island was sketchy, and in a night encircling maneuver two halves of the 87th bumped into each other in the dark. The jumpy recruits fired on each other, causing dozens of casualties in an embarrassing skirmish. It was not a good start.

I wondered how the men felt about such intensive training culminating in disaster. Having looked at the newspaper reports from that era, I knew that the soldiers had been deluged with propaganda about the war in Europe, stories of other soldiers fighting the enemy and dying. Now they had managed only to kill each other in their first botched action.

On the other hand, I mused, it is possible that this relatively safe, if embarrassing, encounter saved their lives.

I had spent some time in the general library stacks, procrastinating about my often-dull research. In my random reading I came across a section on the psychology of killing: soldiers' emotional welfare.

My brief foray into these books told me that the first ten days of battle for green soldiers were very risky. In that time period the men, no matter how well trained, made mistakes as their nerves got the better of them. They were very likely to be killed. I thought to myself, *Darn good thing the enemy had already departed when Lew was out there in the dark.*

I was mad at the army for sending them there in the first place without a decent map.

41

My research took me on a couple of different paths, but I was accustomed to that from working with government documents at the college library. Being at sea in the beginning was normal. There was a lot of history to cover. I wanted to focus on my father's regiment, but the information gleaned from original documents was chaotic: a lot like sorting through his house.

Some general materials could be taken out of the library, but others were in closed stacks. I worked at Lew's house when I could, sitting in his chair, protecting the books from Luigi's incessant chewing, reading constantly to flesh out my understanding of the war. By the end of the week I had a lot more information.

After losing their virginity in the Aleutians, the 87th traveled to Camp Hale, Colorado where they joined ranks with three other regiments, finally forming what would be known as the 10th Mountain Division. Eight thousand soldiers eventually bunked in the mountain valley, smoke from their fires creating a perpetual haze in the normally clear Colorado air.

For the next year the 10th waited and trained. The regular army was inclined to think of them as ski bums in uniform—Eisenhower's "blue-blooded playboys." That spring the Army thought of disbanding the 10th. While the generals vacillated, the discouraged mountaineers summered in Texas, getting used to heat, like all the other soldiers.

Meanwhile in Europe, American forces moved quickly through France, but they stalled in the Italian mountains. When the fall of '44 came the Allies were stuck, repeatedly attempting to capture a few key ridges before winter halted their progress. But there was little progress. The Germans had the high ground, many months to plant mine fields and the leisure to fortify their defenses.

The 10th was finally called to Italy in December of '44.

It appeared that, nothing else having worked, the army was going in for a little blue-blood letting. They assigned the 10th an impossible task as their first mainland action: to attack Riva Ridge, a mile-high summit with a vertical cliff face of two thousand feet. This critical geological fortress had frustrated the regular army for a year. The valley below was a killing field, well-targeted by the Germans perched on top.

The 10th Mountain was still green to combat, but overqualified for everything else about the job. The ascent, in the dark, took ten hours. The Germans, convinced the summit was impenetrable, were caught with their pants down. The 10th's victory was unexpected on both sides. The men carried all the equipment for battle on their backs, but no food. The army had presumed the 10th would fail like everyone else, expecting them dead, or home for dinner. The surprised army transporters learned that getting to the summit was harder than it seemed, subdued Germans or not.

Tired of waiting for supplies on the hill, the 10th scavenged food and immediately pushed for the next big ridge, Belvedere. But this time the Germans were ready and fell back to their well-prepared artillery, mortars, and mine fields. My father's unit had to fight for every inch.

When Belvedere fell the 10th paused to collect its dead. With no transport, the soldiers carried casualties on their backs. I read of one soldier, sent to recover the bodies of his two best friends killed in a foxhole by artillery fire. He found their bodies after days of searching. The men were decomposing, so swollen with gas he could not fit them in body bags. Weeping, he speared them with his bayonet to release the gas so they could be carried down the mountain. I thought of Chuck, his tact with me that first day at the chapel. It seemed a long time ago.

I got up from Lew's chair and patted his box of ashes. He had been there through it all. I wondered what he had seen. The track of my fingers made little dark stains on his cannister. Time was passing and I needed to dust, but remembering Lew's law of houskeeping, I decided against it and instead scratched Luigi's puppy ears while he chewed on my fingers.

42

Dr. Rice was ambitious. She pressed me hard in her frilly office, finishing each session with a satisfied look. It occurred to me that she was in the middle of some primary research of her own. I asked her about it.

She said, "Keep talking and stop asking questions."

"Sieg Heil!"

She might have been pleased, but I was miserable. I felt exposed, like I was going to get in trouble for leaking information. Worse yet, I sounded to myself like a whiner, a crybaby. I gave myself a lot of pep talks. I told Luigi, "She only got my name, rank, and serial number, honest!" He wagged his thick tail and grinned at me.

About eight sessions into therapy Dr. Rice got serious, saying, "I want you in my second women's group. Thursday nights will be better for you, but you are going to have to tell your story and I don't think you're ready to do that in public yet. We'll give it a while. Also, there's a problem with confidentiality because you know someone in that group. Would that bother you?"

"I think it would be okay."

I talked with Dr. Rice one afternoon about my dad and battle fatigue.

She nodded and said, "Those are all common symptoms of stress. That's why I want you in my Thursday night group."

"I was talking about Lew."

"And I was talking about you."

"Okay, what's the group about?"

"It's an abuse survivor's group."

"You think I need that because of getting chased in Colorado Springs?"

She smiled and said, "Denial?"

I must have looked intensely stupid, because after a moment she explained, "I'm not so worried about the incident in Colorado Springs itself. It's why you were there in the first place that worries me. I think you were 'trolling' for punishment on a psychic level. It's a very dangerous behavior; predator males pick up on it instantly. You got away with a cut cheek and a nasty set of flashbacks. When you get some distance and support, the flashbacks will recede."

"How long before they go away entirely?"

"You want the truth?"

I nodded.

"Possibly never. You'll learn to cope with them, know when you're headed for trouble, but there's no magical eraser. You have to *learn* how to not repeat your abuse in your life."

"Like my dad?"

"Kind of. But your dad didn't have help at first. You do."

I joined the support group two weeks before Lew's memorial. I was awash with nerves. Dr. Rice coached me in our last session: "When a new member joins the old members introduce themselves and tell their histories. Then the new member tells her story."

I was nervous. "Can you tell me who I know in the group?"

"I was just about to." And she did.

The group started at eight. Six women filed into the room. The fourth in line was Patrick's mother. She sat down beside me and patted my hand, saying, "I'm glad you're here."

"You knew?"

"Not for sure. I gave you three names."

As Patrick had said, his mother was not stupid.

The stories told that evening will stay in the room. The tales were chilling, making my throat constrict. When my turn finally came I spoke in a whisper, eyes on the ground. The women listened with sympathy, nodding. And then they moved on, speaking of the present. They talked of their lives: children and parents and daily affairs.

I thought about the veterans. I knew why support from people sharing a common experience was both the prevention and the cure for battle fatigue. One plump woman in my group had exclaimed when I spoke of my grandfather, "What a creep! He should at least have waited till you got a chance to settle in!" The group howled with laughter, and she blushed while the woman next to her patted her back and smiled.

Veterans discussing war with civilians was as useful as virgins discussing sex: having never been there, they can't really understand the complexity.

I knew what my next report to T.K. would cover. Battle fatigue.

43

I didn't get to The Lodge to see the historic ski display until the day before it was returned to the library. I parked Lew's Subaru in the shade and left the windows open for Luigi, who was uncrated. He was slowly learning not to chew everything, but I took out my backpack.

I walked toward the building in whose upper floors I had been born. I passed several ducks swimming in a round pond. Their pool was circled by a drive that led to the huge overhang, protecting the formal entrance to the Sun Valley Lodge. A very short doorman in his sixties greeted me pleasantly. As I walked toward the wide doors, he ushered me in, smiling. I thanked him.

The opulent lobby of the old resort was sparsely staffed in the off-season by maids in calf-length blue dresses. The occasional bathrobed tourist shuffled below the sign advertising the spa. In the middle of the lobby, in front of a large fireplace, a group of glass-topped display tables housed the historic collection.

These tables secreted a lot of documents that I probably could have used, as well as a huge quantity of pictures. I looked at the photos, set in chronological order: the resort under construction in the twenties; the thirties whisking by with smiling Austrian ski instructors teaching rich-looking women; the early forties housing convalescing veterans; the mid-forties seeing the return of a thin and grim group of new ski teachers.

I looked at the veterans' young and lined faces, presenting a sharp contrast to their knickered Austrian predecessors and money-polished students. One photo caught my eye. A rescue scene, the group of skiers standing on the mountainside. The picture showed Lew. I knew it immediately because the photo was in Lew's house as well. He was belaying a presumably injured person on a stretcher. I admired his stance again, rooted to the slippery slope, rope about his waist, a taut link to the stretcher.

I noticed something that I had missed before. He looked casual, almost relaxed, at home with the tension of the line. I wondered why he didn't seem worried, with an injured person counting on his balance.

I had just started to read the caption when I felt someone standing behind me. I turned and looked down to find the smiling doorman. He was watching me and moved a bit closer as I turned. He directed his attention to the photograph.

"Know what they were doing?"

"No."

"There'd been a plane wreck on the back side of Baldy. Benni sent the ski patrol up to have a look. Took them a day or two to find the wreckage. But it wouldn't have mattered—there wasn't much left of anyone after the crash."

"They were dead?"

"The moment the plane found the mountain."

I looked at the short man, thinking, *That's why Lew looks so casual. They were transporting a corpse: familiar territory.*

I asked, "Did you know anyone on the patrol?"

"All of them."

"Lew Pierce?"

"Right there." The man pointed to my father on the belay line.

"That's my father."

"Holy shit!" he said. Then he stuck out a hand and said, "Cecil Andrews. Can we sit down?"

"I'd like that."

"Let me just tell them at the desk. I'm due for a break anyway." He hurried off and returned as rapidly.

I remained silent as he seated himself, a little embarrassed now by my forwardness, and not sure how to proceed. But I underestimated the congeniality of my companion. He started talking right away. "You're Lew's little girl. I haven't seen you since you were shorter than me by a long shot." He gestured at knee height with his hand. "How's your mother?"

"Fine."

"We were all real sorry to hear about Lew. I'll be at the memorial."

"Thanks. That would be nice. How well did you know my father?"

"Real well. We grew up in the same town. My older brother, Bud, went off to war with Lew. They were lucky to come home together too."

"Where is Bud now?"

"He died last year. Heart trouble."

"I'm sorry."

"He'd been sick for a long time, but we were all pretty broken up about it anyway. That was before Lew found out about his cancer. I think he felt deserted. They were good friends. It's been a tough year."

"I know it. How long have you been here?"

"Sun Valley? Almost forty years. I'm going to retire next year and take my wife someplace where there's less snow in the winter. All that textured weather is fine when you can ski on it, but otherwise it just makes for a lot of work."

"I guess so. Were you in the war too?"

"I was too young. Bud wrote to me back East after he and Lew got here. Said there was lots of work. I took the train out and I've worked at the bell desk ever since."

"You must have seen a lot."

"You bet I've seen a lot. A lot of tourists, a lot of veterans, a lot of things that never should have happened."

I changed the subject. "I'm doing a report for school on the 10th Mountain and I was thinking of branching off onto shell shock for my second paper. You're the only person I've talked to that knew my father before the war. Your brother too. Was there a lot of difference between them before and after the war?"

He looked at me as if I were dimwitted, but responded pleasantly enough.

"Well, that's a mouthful, but I know what you're getting at. After the war they took some terrible risks. It was like they had seen all life had. The rest didn't matter. And they drank like fish; that didn't help. My brother Bud was even worse than your dad, and Lew was no saint when it came to alcohol."

"Did they drink before the war?"

"Sure as hell not like after the war. Your dad was just a regular guy before he went away. A little too proud of his skiing, but pretty much a regular guy. When he came home there was nothing he wouldn't stop at. I remember one story of them in the summer, Bud and Lew and a bunch of the patrol. I was home with my wife."

"What did they do?"

"This one night they went drinking in Stanley. That's over the pass to the north. When the bars closed they got the idea they could drive Lew's car on the old cat tracks over Galena and get home a bit quicker. They got more than halfway back, well over the summit, but coming down this side on the switchbacks they found a big tree over the road. They were within an hour of home and they didn't want to go back, so Lew tried to drive around the damn thing. The station wagon got stuck and started to teeter on the edge of the slope. All the guys got out but your dad. He stayed behind the wheel."

"What happened?"

"While Lew sat in front, the other guys went around and lowered the tailgate. They took a seat on the back, while the front rocked over the side of the cliff. If they turned around they could see the switchback looping around down the ravine. Well, they passed the bottle back and forth through the back seat to Lew, most of them still sitting on the trunk. Every now and then one got up to take a pee and the car would tip further. Then he'd come back and sit down again and it would steady up some.

"After a while Lew, still at the wheel, talked them into letting him try to drive the thing down the hill onto the next piece of road. Well, they were pretty drunk and by the time they got done with another fifth, it looked like a pretty good idea. Lew told them he'd aim for right between these two big trees at the base and then turn right onto the road.

"They didn't want to just walk off and leave the car to slide down the hill on its own. They didn't get paid that much, you see? They wanted to keep the car."

"Right."

"So, they asked Lew if he was ready, and he said yes. So all the guys stood up off the tailgate at once. And down he went."

"What happened?"

"Well, he aimed okay, right square between the trees. The only trouble was the gap was about four inches too narrow for the car, so it rocketed down the hill and wedged itself like a cork in between those two trees."

"What happened to my dad?"

"He was fine. He said he'd just as soon sleep in the car as walk back for a chainsaw, so the rest of them walked back into town about daylight, got a saw and walked back. I guess he was pretty peevish that they didn't bring him a thermos of coffee. But they got the car out."

"What did you think of my dad?"

"Hell of a nice guy when he wasn't blind drunk and pissed as the devil."

"Did he have a temper before the war?"

"Lew? Not much. But then, he didn't drink before he went away."

"Did Lew have trouble with all women, or just my mother?"

"The ladies loved Lew, but they didn't love that they couldn't own him. He didn't take orders well after the war. He said he'd had enough of that for one lifetime. He was just so damn good at what he did, people generally let him go do it. Wasn't easy on the ladies, though."

"He never married again?"

"He said once was enough."

"Oh."

44

When I left the lodge I knew for certain when my dad took to drinking. It might have seemed obvious to anyone else, but having always thought it was a character flaw, I was relieved. I headed back to the library, patting Luigi. I knew by now exactly where to look, and I read for all of what remained of the afternoon.

Most of the technical works on battle fatigue were dry and unappealing. I had to force myself to continue. The authors seemed bent on hiding the facts in a maze of language. I went to the psychology section as well as the military history section. After a while I managed to unravel what seemed like a plausible hypothesis.

The army claimed that World War II veterans did not suffer from Post-Traumatic Stress Syndrome. But even though the official word was that it did not exist, other documents told me that toward the end of the second world war more soldiers were sent home from battle fatigue than enlisting agents could replace with new recruits.

The psychological effects of battle had many different names. The researchers agreed, however, that after only one month's combat, emotional maiming would begin. I read this with a chill, afraid for my dad, thinking that he might have used up his ration of nerves when the war was far from over.

The brief efficiency expected of warriors surprised me. Every day in battle was like a clock ticking, not just for their survival, but for their ultimate competency. The army worried about this: trained soldiers were necessary, and expensive to replace. If properly maintained, they could be used longer in battle. For efficiency's sake they needed mental breaks, time out of danger, preferably in the company of their immediate friends, their unit.

Four days at the front, then four days at the rear lines seemed to be the magic number for prevention of emotional exhaustion and resultant absenteeism. Using this recipe, the British had kept men in battle for six months before they went crazy. The army calculated things like that. To make it work you had to have enough soldiers, and you had to keep them together.

Didn't function so well, when all but one died, I thought.

According to the experts, PTSD, shell shock, was "a reaction to psychologically traumatic events outside the range of normal human experience. Manifestations of PTSD include recurrent and intrusive dreams, flashbacks, uncontrolled recollections of the experience, and emotional blunting."

Emotional blunting, I thought. *Interesting phrase.*

The text continued: "Social withdrawal and exceptional difficulty or reluctance in initiating or maintaining intimate relationships are common. Sleep disturbances are commonplace: bad dreams, night terrors and insomnia."

I wasn't sure how I could ignore that close of a description.

Nor was I sure how the army could ignore it. The words could have been a diary. I wondered how many people were in the same boat. The following passage reiterated what I already knew: "These symptoms in turn lead to serious difficulties in adjustment, resulting in self-medication, alcoholism, divorce and unemployment. The symptoms may linger for months or years after the trauma, often emerging after a long delay."

There was not much mention from the army about what happened to the fatigued soldiers after the war was over. I guessed they figured as long as their veterans didn't kill a bunch of civilians it wasn't their problem. The military was clearly more interested in the mechanics of keeping soldiers functioning as killers during the conflict than they were about bringing them home with psyches intact. Understandable: unless you happened to need one of those soldiers for something later on, like being your dad, why bother? I wondered briefly if my father could have rescued me from my fate on the East coast if he had not been so mad.

But then, I was pretty mad myself by this point. I gathered up my notes and left the library, furious. The list of wrongdoers was lengthy: the army who threw the mountaineers into an impossible situation; the resort that used the talent of the returning veterans in return for poverty wages; the veterans' administration for promising to take care of my dad, then threatening to take his house, leaving him alone to die. *Seemed like the army didn't send search parties to the hillside for remains of their dead anymore.*

I got into the car and slammed the door. Luigi thought this was funny and wagged his tail while chewing the battered stick shift.

"Stop that!" I said.

He licked my hand and looked longingly at the projecting window handles.

"It's an addiction," I told him.

He wagged his tail.

I patted him.

As we drove through town I thought of my distant family. I was still in a foul mood when we got home, thinking longingly of search parties.

45

One afternoon, not long after I talked with Cecil Andrews at the lodge, I was looking for wood glue to repair the face of a cabinet. I rummaged through the shelves in the garage. Not hidden, but stacked behind a group of adhesives, I found a box of photos.

Judy had told me Lew lived in the garage when he first bought the lot. The backs of the shelves held many odd treasures, so this was not a surprise. I opened the box and sifted through the photos. To the side lay a thin leather box, about the size of a checkbook. I opened it and then I was surprised, because sliding to the corner was a medal, hanging from a ribbon. I picked it up. My father's bronze star lay in my hand.

I thought of my own ribbons, embarrassments because they did not match the sacrifice required of me to earn them, important mostly to others. But I was proud of him. I carried the thin metal star inside with the pictures and placed it next to one of his framed ski shots. Then I looked at the photos.

They were snapshots, pictures from a soldier's camera during the war. The photos showed what looked like Italy's Po Valley, green and lush with spring, which failed to shut down, even in wartime. In one series, a mountain pond hosted a naked soldier, thin and spare, dousing himself and smiling. Another man fished with a makeshift line.

A few pictures lower a German soldier lay dead. By this time I knew some about the Po valley, but it was a shock to see the snapshots, sitting boxed like any family memorabilia. But then, they were Lew's family pictures, I suppose. I loaded the box of pictures and Luigi into the car. Then I headed back to the library, intent on comparing the pictures with the ones I had seen in the history books.

I got there and waved at my librarian, sitting behind her desk working at her own unknown research. She smiled at me as I disappeared into the stacks. The pictures of the Po Valley matched: the same hills, the same river, a sign in the town for the drugstore. Flipping through one volume, I came across an account of the 10th's campaign in the Po again. I read it twice and assembled the story in my mind.

The Po valley lies north of Riva Ridge and Mount Belvedere. It is traversed by the similarly named river, whose headwaters originate in the Alps.

In late April, 1945, after the 10th Mountain had chased the Germans from Riva Ridge, Hitler's troops dug into the south-facing slope of the Po valley. There they waited for their pursuers. The mountaineers were moving fast on their way north, still outrunning their supply lines. Worried American pilots bombed the Germans' defenses, but the enemy went to ground, emerging when the planes departed to fight from trenches on the hillsides, shelling their attackers with terrific firepower. It took a week for the 10th to push across the Po River, leaving over a thousand members killed or maimed on its banks.

Still traveling north after the retreating Germans, remnants of the 10th neared Lake Garda. Advanced units filed into rail tunnels cut in the hills. On the other side, the Germans depressed their cannons and fired point-blank down the rail lines. The concussion, condensed by the tunnel, tore the leading American soldiers to pieces. A sniper, possibly my father, was quickly dispatched over the hill to deal with the enemy cannon crew. The remaining soldiers averted their eyes in the tunnel hours later, quietly walking past the blood-soaked jumble of arms and legs. The tunnel reeked with the viscera of their unrecognizable friends, killed within sight of victory.

With no choice but to continue, the 10th moved further north, fighting house to house, not in a mood to take prisoners. Demoralized Germans began surrendering in such numbers that there were not enough troops to guard them. Leaving the prisoners to walk back to the rear lines on their own, the battered 10th prepared to push north once more, but on May 2nd, as they prepared to leave, the news of the German army's surrender in Italy flowed through the camp.

Peculiarly, there was no rejoicing; the division as a whole sat down and wept.

My father was the only man of his unit to live through the fifty days of more or less continuous fighting.

I sat at the table with Lew's pictures, thinking of the last action, the sobbing warriors.

Shortly after, the librarian walked up to me, a folder in hand. She said, "I thought you might like to see this." I took it from her and thanked her.

The file was thin, about twenty Xeroxed pages, marked halfway with a Post-it note indicating a passage. I opened it. In an interview with soldiers of the 10th, Lew Pierce was one of the subjects. I stared at the marked page, silenced, as if he were talking to me.

He had been asked about his career as a sniper with the 10th.

Lew said simply, "It's not hard being a sniper. You're a long way from the man you kill. And he most probably deserved it.

"But it *is* hard to be in front. There's nothing worse than leading a group of men in mined territory. Bombs underfoot are much scarier than overhead. You have to walk separately when you are moving a division, so if it goes badly you are always alone. At first it is so quiet; you walk through the mines like they're not there. If you knew they were there, you sure as hell wouldn't walk through them!

"Then you hear explosions behind you. You want to run. You can hear men screaming, and you want to go back, to help, or escape, or whatever. But you cannot go back over the land you came from, nor can you stay still, waiting for your friends to catch up. *They may never catch up.* No matter how frightened you are, at some point you will have to move again.

"In a field of mines there is no louder sound than the next step you take. Let me tell you, it's not brave to go forward, when you cannot go back. Bravery is the moment you make the choice to move at all."

I put the paper down, my fingers still touching the page.

I remembered the blue doors, my father's determined passing, leaving me the product of the years we did not share. Lew offered me the chance to move. I looked down at my arms, the faint scars of self-destruction in view. I was ashamed, thinking Lew would have expected better of me. I knew now for whom he had waited. And hoped.

Humbled, I put the folder on the box of pictures he'd left.

The librarian looked at the folder and nodded as I went out. I'd show her the photos another day.

46

I slowly came to accept my mother's thorough silence. The abrupt end of her impermanent affection left me chilled. But unlike my mother I was ambivalent. Some days the phone beckoned me to call, beg her to love me again. But even if it hadn't been futile, the call commanded a price I now refused to pay. Remembering my grandfather's voice, hissing relentlessly down the wires, I wondered what would have happened if she had simply hung up.

So I sat, patient, stubborn and lonely, encouraged by my father's fine example, writing endless drafts for T.K. Eventually, I let the phone lie still with a quieter mind. I *hoped* my mother would catch up. But that was different than walking back through the mine field to get her.

The next move was possibly harder, and *required* a phone call.

The day I decided to take Lew back up the mountain, his hollyhocks were knee high. To frustrate Luigi's mission of mass destruction, I left him crated at Lew's place, whining and scratching in his puppy prison. I would have liked to have had him along, but a pup of that age is not equipped for such a hike.

The walk to Exhibition was brutal. The series of ski runs leading there directly were too steep for me to climb. The more gentle ascending cat tracks offered an alternate, but much longer route. I traversed the many switchbacks, constantly climbing through the trees, Lew's sturdily-housed remains switched from arm to arm. It took a good three hours and many breathless stops, looking back over the valley. I saw trees scratched by bear twenty feet up. I thought of them, standing on the winter snow pack common to these parts.

The trail flattened along the last section before Exhibition.

The walk was easier now. The open bowls of Bald Mountain waited still higher, but that trip would be accomplished some other day.

I continued past a sign directing timid skiers to other trails and carried Lew's ashes to the edge of Exhibition.

I looked over the slope, imagining Lew, in his snow cat long ago, looking down for the man with the pole to guide him through the drifts. I could see him in my mind, accelerating in front of the landslide of snow. I leaned over the edge of the nearly vertical drop. The wind from the valley beyond hit my face and brushed by. You could almost see Lew's house from here, behind the bend in the river.

I sat down on the shale and watched the lowlands, listening to the wind.

After a few moments I opened the cannister of my father's ashes. Our last journey together was at an end. I pushed my hands through his silken and gritty remains.

The wind took the fragments from me. The clear air wafted the particles in a delicate, sun-refined cloud, swirling over the crest of the summit; the larger hung there, poised for another descent, while the current shaped the smaller for a moment as they dispersed, lofting higher and finally out of sight.

The walk back through the switchbacks seemed too long. The shady side of the slope was still clothed in a massive snowdrift. I walked over to it and sat, looking over the edge. The snow was crystalline, a gleaming highway to the valley. With a little push I sent myself over, skidding and sliding down the glacier, the drifts bucking under my seat like a spirited horse.

As I drove back through town alone, I thought about what Patrick's mother had quoted to me days ago: "Death ends a life, not a relationship." She was a smart woman.

When I got back to the house Patrick's car was in the drive.

He stood in the doorway, stepping out when I arrived, looking uncertain. Then he smiled.

I got out of Lew's car, finally in motion. I ran to meet him, wet, clean and dusty.

"God, you're soggy," he said, catching his balance, taking my face in his hands, smiling. "I got your message. Try again?"

"Yes."

The End.

ACKNOWLEDGMENTS

My thanks to all who have helped so much; Noel and Nick for tirelessly living with a grouchy typist; Keith and Anna Quincy for their tremendous support and encouragement; Pip Shepley and my brother Chip for inspiration and permission; my editors, Joanie Eppinga and Gerri Sombke for their incredible attention to detail.

I would also like to thank The Wood River Journal and Ed Scott for his words from the article, "Sun Valley's Best Skier," published on January 23rd, 1990 in Ketchum Idaho.

Last but not least I want to thank my dedicated champions of the common reader: Sima Thorpe, Ron McComb, Dan Tynan, Phyllis Mast, Laurie Baldwin, Sally Sovey, Debbie Cameron, and Poo Pulliam who all read the manuscript before it was much fun to do so!

This is a work of fiction: any resemblance to any persons living or dead is purely coincidental.

SELECTED BIBLIOGRAPHY

Soldiers on Skis —a Pictorial Memoir of the 10th Mountain Division by Whitlock and Bishop. Published in 1992 by Paladine Press, Copyright 1992 by Flint Whitlock and Bob Bishop.

On Killing—the Psychological Cost Of Learning to Kill in War and Society. By Dave Grossman, edited by G. Kloske. Published by Little Brown and Company, November 1996.

Article, "Sun Valley's Best Skier," by Ed Scott, published March 23, 1990 in *The Wood River Journal.*

The 10th Mountain Division website and many copies of "Blizzard" the official newsletter of the 10th Mountain Division.